FINDING HOPE

ELIZABETH JOHNS

Copyright © 2024 by Elizabeth Johns
Cover Design by 17 Studio Book Design
Edited by Scott Moreland
Historical content by Heather King

ISBN: 978-1960794260

All rights reserved.
No part of this book may be reproduced in any form or by any electronic or mechanical means, including information storage and retrieval systems, without written permission from the author, except for the use of brief quotations in a book review.

CHAPTER 1

Hope Whitford had watched that morning as her elder sister Faith had married Dominic, Lord Westwood, their guardian, and not without a little trepidation. Nothing would change, they said, but Hope was sceptical. She now sat at a table littered with remnants of the wedding breakfast, watching as Dominic danced with Faith, the two of them looking as though nothing or no one else existed in the world.

Hope could not suppress some jealousy towards Lord Westwood. She was not proud of this emotion, but it was difficult to think of Faith as anything other than her motherly elder sister and best friend. She had not even wanted to come to London and had had no thoughts of getting married, yet she had made the match of the Season. It was not that Hope wasn't pleased for her sister, but she did not want everything to change. But how could it not?

She looked around the ballroom, which no longer resembled the heavens as it had only a few weeks before at her and her sister's debut ball. Instead, it looked like a rose garden with tables for dining and room for dancing. Mr. Cunningham was doting on Joy and Freddy Tiger as the beloved rescued cat was currently taking turns jumping from her lap to his. Hope laughed as she thought of the cat's performance during the ceremony, when he'd leaped from Joy's pocket to pounce on Faith's train as it had snaked along behind her. The congregation had not been able to contain their laughter.

Patience was surrounded by her court of gentlemen in Regimentals. They all looked the same to Hope except for Major Stuart. He at least, with his fair features, resembled his brother Lord Westwood enough that she recognized him.

Lord Montford, another of Lord Westwood's close friends, was holding out his hand, clearly asking Grace to dance. Hope stabbed her confit de canard with her fork, chewed it without tasting it, then took a long swallow of her champagne.

"May I join you?" Lord Carew, also one of Westwood's friends, asked as he slid into the seat beside her before she could answer. "You look as though you are in mourning rather than celebrating."

Hope tried not to watch as Lord Rotham twirled the beautiful Vivienne Cunningham around the room. She was Freddy, Mr. Cunningham's younger sister and every bit as beautiful. With her blond curls she was the complete opposite of Hope, and looked ethereal next to Rotham's dangerous dark looks.

"Would it help if we danced?" Carew asked, as if reading her thoughts.

"I doubt it."

"Which sister will be next, do you think?" the Dowager asked the now Dowager Lady Westwood none too quietly—at least, from where Hope sat, it seemed as though she was almost shouting.

"It is hard to say. All of them have plenty of suitors."

Hope heard a harrumph. "Better catch Rotham for the next one."

Her ears pricked at the name.

"He will have to want to be caught. I am not certain that will happen anytime soon."

"Balderdash! He will want what his friends have, mark my words."

Hope frowned at that. What a lowering thought. To be wanted only for such a reason.

"Come. You need to dance." Carew held out his hand to her, and she accepted it, meeting his twinkling blue eyes.

"Perhaps you are right."

"My attentions to your sister seemed to get Westwood's notice. Maybe Rotham will wake up and notice the prize before him as well."

As she was swept into his arms, Hope thought perhaps she had fallen for the wrong man.

"Smile, dearest," Lord Carew said as they danced. "Nothing will get Rotham's attention more than seeing you enjoying another man's arms."

"Forgive me," Hope said. "I must be a terrible partner."

"Not at all," he said graciously.

"Why are you doing this for me?"

"It would amuse me to see Rotham brought to heel."

"Did it amuse you to do the same to Westwood?"

He smiled devilishly. "Indeed it did."

He was remarkably handsome. Why could she not be in love with him? But Grace, her younger sister, was very much enamoured of the Irish rogue and Hope did not wish to hurt her.

"Were you insincere in your offer for Faith, then?" she asked.

"Not insincere, no, but I knew it would have the desired effect."

"Gentlemen are odd creatures," she replied.

"Men feel the same way about the fair sex. It keeps things interesting."

Hope allowed her gaze to slide to Rotham and Miss Cunningham.

"I would not do that if I were you," he cautioned.

"Why not?" Hope asked, though she knew she should keep her eyes on her partner. "What is the harm in looking?"

He shook his head sadly. "You have much to learn, *mo stór.*"

Hope bristled to defend herself.

"It is human nature to want what you cannot have, do you not agree?" he asked.

"So you are saying if he thinks he cannot have me, then he will want me?"

"Precisely."

She shook her head. "And you say you are not odd creatures."

"Smile, my dear. He is looking this way."

Hope smiled her biggest smile and laughed.

Lord Carew touched a finger to her cheek and boldly caressed it.

"What are you doing?" she asked through the smile, which was so wide it almost hurt.

"Trust me."

"Making me look like a hussy is your idea of making him jealous?"

Lord Carew laughed and bowed as the dance ended. He held out his arm to her, then escorted her from the floor. Hope could not help but see Lord Rotham and Miss Cunningham speaking with his mother, the Duchess.

"It is no secret Miss Cunningham is the Duchess's choice for Rotham," Carew said quietly in her ear. "They have been intended for each other from a young age, though nothing was made formal, I understand."

"How am I to compete with that?" she asked, as much to herself as to him.

"You don't," he said.

"I don't understand."

"It is not you versus Miss Cunningham," he explained. "That is the wrong way to look at it, and will only bring animosity between you."

"So I am to befriend her?" she asked sceptically.

"If you must, but at least do not hold this against her. She may not wish for the match herself. Regardless of any affection they may feel, men do not enjoy cattish females with petty, bitter tendencies."

"I cannot say I enjoy them myself," she muttered. Instead of returning her to her table, Lord Carew kept walking. "Where are you taking me?"

"Have you had the privilege of being introduced to the Duchess?"

"No, but now is not the time." Hope tried to resist and pull back.

"Nonsense. No time like the present!"

Hope suspected Carew had his own reasons for doing this to her, but Rotham had seen them coming, and it was too late to draw back.

He looked as darkly handsome as ever, and Hope prayed that her reaction to him was not outwardly obvious. She still clung to Lord Carew's arm, and hoped she wasn't bruising him.

Hope noticed the Duchess stop her conversation and look Hope over from head to toe with pursed lips and a disapproving gleam in her eye. She was probably in her mid-forties and striking—or would have been were she not looking so censorious.

"Carew, Miss Whitford." Rotham bowed. "Mother, have you had the privilege of meeting Miss Whitford?"

"I have not," she replied tartly, in a tone that said she would rather not ever have that privilege.

"Mother, Sister. This is Miss Whitford. Miss Whitford, this is my mother, the Duchess of Davenmere, and my younger sister, Lady Claudia."

Hope curtsied, but deliberately not low enough for royalty. She would not toady to one who felt her consequence so strongly. The Duchess was not tall, but her presence was all intimidation. Hope barely noticed Lady Claudia beside the wrathful stare of the mother.

"Are you acquainted with Miss Cunningham? She has been Rotham's intended from the cradle," the Duchess returned.

Hope smiled her sweetest smile and curtsied to the beautiful girl. "It is a pleasure, Miss Cunningham," she said.

She returned the courtesy, which made Hope like her a little, even against her wishes. It was hard to hate someone who was kind. Perhaps Carew was correct that Miss Cunningham was not the enemy.

"You are new in Town, are you not?" she asked in a soft, angelic voice. "My brother has mentioned you and your sisters."

"Yes, we lived a secluded life near Bath with Lady Halbury until Lord Westwood became our guardian."

"I believe my brother invited you to our garden party. I do hope you will attend."

"How very kind. I will consult with the Dowager. I do believe my sister and her husband are preparing to say farewell. If you'll excuse me?"

Hope began to pull away, but Carew stayed with her as she walked away. "The Duchess has thrown down the gauntlet, has she not? Rotham will not be pleased."

"He is a grown man. If he chooses to allow his mother to lead him around by the nose, that is his choice."

"She is a dragon," Carew agreed good-naturedly.

"Miss Cunningham is lovely." So lovely that it hurt Hope to compare herself to the young lady.

"Rotham sees her as a sister."

Hope stopped. "It matters not. I am resolved not to wear my heart on my sleeve."

"Good girl," Carew said with an approving smile.

Hope only wished she felt as resolved in her heart as in her mind.

MAX WATCHED Miss Whitford walk away on Carew's arm, and it was difficult not to go after her. A strange sensation of jealousy pulsed through his veins, but he dared not show any hints of affection lest his mother try to destroy Miss Whitford. He had no right to monopolize her and, at this point, he was not ready to acknowledge more than a genteel friendship.

The Duchess was ruthless in trying to get her way—as witnessed by the announcement she had just made.

"I will call on you to discuss this in the morning, your Grace. Miss Cunningham." He made a curt bow to both of them, then left the wedding breakfast.

What he hated the most was that Vivienne was caught between he and his mother. Max had been brought up by the Duchess and knew she would do anything to have her way. Vivienne knew his family, but not the lengths his mother would go to, either to be right or get what she wanted.

Her determination had come between them more than once, and Max refused to let her run his life, nor make such monumental decisions for him.

Max dismissed his carriage and walked home. Part of him hoped he would be set upon by footpads because he was itching for a fight. It was not even dark yet when he left, though he scarcely noticed his surroundings. He did not go to one of his clubs that night, but passed them without going inside. Instead of returning home, he walked and walked, considering the matter.

Besides being twelve years his junior, Vivienne was like a little sister to him, and he could no more consider marrying her than his own flesh and blood. Thankfully, Vivienne understood, and professed to feel the same. However, his mother saying such things in public would only harm Vivienne. He must—would—put a stop to her madness, once and for all. Unfortunately, short of matricide, the only way to stop her from spreading the falsehood was to marry someone else.

He no more wanted to be forced into marriage than to marry Vivienne—or allow his mother to have her way. It was difficult to honour thy mother when she was behaving dishonourably.

Max could not even say how long he wandered the streets, but he did eventually find himself back at his town house.

The next morning, he had had time to calm himself, and he dressed whilst mentally preparing for battle. To what lengths would he have to go to see his mother surrender?

He donned his beaver hat and took his walking stick from Baxter, then proceeded across Grosvenor Square to his parents' house. His future residence. His father stayed buried in the country unless he had to come to London, but would he trouble himself to rein in the Duchess if Max asked? Max shook his head, answering his own question. He was a grown man and had to deal with this himself.

The door opened before he could knock.

"Good morning, my lord," Evans said and held out his hand for Max's hat and walking stick.

"Evans." Max acknowledged the long-time family retainer. "Where is her Grace?"

"I believe she is still in her chambers, my lord. Her maid sent down word that she was abed with the headache."

"I will show myself up, then," he said before Evans could protest.

Her Grace did not care to be disturbed in her chambers, but Max knew this was one of her tricks to fob him off. She knew full well he would be there this morning, and was trying to disconcert him. It would not work.

He climbed the stairs with deliberate patience, forcing himself to be calm, then knocked on the door to her sitting room—he did not care to find her in dishabille, after all.

"Enter," she called, very likely expecting a servant.

He opened the door and found her fully dressed, sitting near the window.

"Rotham," she greeted him coolly.

"Your Grace." He walked forward and kissed her on the cheek to discompose her. "You are looking well."

"I have an announcement en route to the papers. Vivienne and her parents have agreed it is for the best to make things formal."

Max sat down and slowly crossed his legs. He had anticipated something as base as this. He could somewhat relate to Westwood's fury when Sir Julian had made such an announcement about Westwood's wife, except now it was his own mother trying to force his hand publicly.

"Have you nothing to say?" she demanded.

"I think it is unfortunate that you felt you had the power to do such a thing. I have already made it clear to the papers that any such announcement, unless delivered personally by me, is not to be printed or such publication will result in serious consequences for them."

She drew in a gasp with anger.

"I will not be forced into marrying Miss Cunningham, or anyone else, your Grace."

"You intend to be entrapped by that vulgar Whitford girl!"

"No one will entrap me, including you. I will marry whom I want, when I want."

"But this has been arranged for years!" she argued.

"There is nothing binding and you know it. Vivienne and I never agreed to such an arrangement. Besides, if that were the case, you would not have invited half a dozen ladies to your house party."

"A house party that you promised to be at, and rather than honour that obligation, you went hunting instead!"

"I made no promises."

"How can you be so unfeeling?" His mother's voice shook with anger.

"I could ask the same of you."

"You were brought up to be a dutiful son. You cannot marry whomever you wish like your friends do. You must honour your name and title!"

"I have no intention of besmirching the dukedom with a guttersnipe, your Grace."

"Yet you hang in the pocket of one! Do you think I do not see your name associated with hers in the papers every day?"

"Miss Whitford is a lady."

"Ha! She is gentry at best."

"I will not argue this, your Grace."

"Vivienne has everything you could ever want—birth, fortune, looks. She is a diamond of the first water!"

"She is as a sister to me."

"You have raised expectations in her breast! As well as her parents and yours!"

"My father has no opinion on the matter whatsoever. This is solely your doing."

"There you are wrong." She pushed a letter across the table towards him, and Max recognized his father's script and seal.

Max picked it up and tossed it into the fire. "You have bullied him into proclaiming his deepest wish for the union, have you not? It will not work."

"Then you will be cut off."

"So be it. I cannot be removed as heir. I can survive until then."

He stood and made her a bow—he would give her no reason to disclaim him a gentleman at least.

"You will regret this!" she called after him.

Once he was out of sight of Davenmere House, Max increased his pace.

He yelled for his secretary the moment he was through the door. "Johnson, the Duchess has been busy. Hand deliver a notice to all the papers at once! No announcements are to be published unless at my expressed wish!"

The nerve of his mother! She was correct in one thing, though—Vivienne was beautiful, but in a girlish, innocent sort of way. Miss Whitford's deep blue eyes flashed fire and held promise of hidden depths that were yet to be explored.

CHAPTER 2

*H*ope dressed for the Cunningham garden party in a subdued morning gown of jonquil muslin adorned with tiny embroidered daisies. She paired it with a straw bonnet with a white ribbon and daisies to match. She was determined to think of Miss Cunningham as Freddy's sister, and not Rotham's intended. Hope adored Freddy Cunningham, so why not his sister?

"You look plucked straight from a meadow," Joy teased. She was the only one waiting in their sitting room. Little Freddy Tiger was no longer so little, and was currently attacking the tassels on one of the sofa pillows.

"Stop that, Freddy!" Joy scolded as she picked him up and moved him.

"It is a garden party," Hope retorted. "You are certain you do not wish to go? The invitation expressly included you."

"I am certain that was Mr. Cunningham's doing, but I do not think I feel up to watching everybody else be gay and playing games and not be able to participate."

"Shall I stay here with you? I do not mind."

"Miss Hillier has promised to finish reading *Evelina* to me, and Westwood's chef has promised to make me some jam tarts."

Hope shook her head. "Very well, but you must assure me you will take some fresh air. I do not think it is healthy to stay inside all the time."

"Easily done. I am good about taking Freddy out myself."

Patience and Grace came into the room, wearing rose and green muslin respectively.

"Shall we go?" Patience asked. "The Dowager will be waiting for us."

They did not have far to go. The Cunninghams' town house abutted the Green Park, and tents and tables had been set up, along with several lawn games from tennis to lawn bowls for those who wished for amusement.

The formal garden was lined with yew trees that had been shaped into ovals, surrounding a large fountain as the centrepiece. Flowering hedges formed the outer boundaries with plane and oak trees for shade, while blooms of lavender and rose filled the air with their perfume. Their bright colours danced gaily before the sombre green of the hedge.

Hope was trying to put a sunny smile on her face, but she felt only melancholy. Her best friend and sister was married and gone, and Rotham, whose friendship she had taken for granted when he was escorting her everywhere for her safety, now appeared to be unattainable. Why had he never mentioned he was already betrothed?

Not only had she lost a friend, she had also foolishly allowed herself to become enamoured with him. Had his seeming interest in her only been feigned or due to proximity?

"Welcome!" Freddy Cunningham said warmly when he saw them arrive. "Did Miss Joy not come?" He looked and sounded disappointed.

"I am afraid not. She thought seeing everyone else enjoying themselves would be too much temptation."

"I'd have thought she would enjoy the sunshine and the company." He frowned.

"Perhaps it is too soon. Besides, Westwood's chef promised her some pastries, and the governess was to entertain her with some letters of Frances Burney."

"I pray that is all it is. Have you met my sister?"

"I have had the pleasure," Hope replied, turning to the young lady who had joined them. "How do you do?"

"I am so glad you could join us, Miss Whitford," she said with a kind smile.

"We were pleased to come. Your home and garden are lovely."

Mr. Cunningham introduced his sister to Patience and Grace, with whom she was of an age. They seemed to take to each other immediately, and began giggling about something.

Hope began to feel ancient, and wondered if she'd ever been that young. Miss Cunningham seemed so very young and innocent—the very opposite of Lord Rotham. He would eat her alive or be bored to tears by her. He needed someone who could keep his interest. Yet, that was not to be Hope. It chafed that she was not thought to be good enough for the likes of a future duke, but that was the way of the world, and she did not wish to be the cause of any strife or viewed as an object of disdain by his family. Hope had always borne this strong need to be liked. Perhaps it came with being the second child and one of many siblings, yet she did not detect this weakness in any of her sisters.

It was hard not to think about what Lord Carew had said about wanting what was unattainable. She certainly felt that effect on herself. However, she had to behave indifferently for her own protection. What was the distinction between indifference and coldness, though? After he'd protected her and been her friend, she owed Rotham better than that. She'd heard some say that men and women could not be just friends. It was not always true, certainly, but it could be more difficult.

Hope knew the moment he arrived. The hairs on her arms and neck seemed to prickle with awareness. Instead of looking for him, she searched for Lord Carew, who, when her eyes met his, smiled at her with amusement.

He began walking towards her. "Do you have need of me, Miss Whitford?"

She put her chin up in the air, offended that she had been called out. "I did no such thing, but now that you are here, you can be useful."

"At your service, of course. Are we pretending indifference?"

She tilted her head and pursed her lips. "I was trying to decide how to accomplish indifference while remaining friendly. Is such a thing possible? He did do me and my sisters a great service. All of you did."

He inclined his head. "I do not think you need to be uncivil or cold, but do not go out of your way. Make him come to you."

"But how do I behave when I am with him?"

"Treat him like you treat me. Although you should not pretend to be indifferent with me," he added.

"This is terribly confusing. I do not think I can do it. Besides, what is the point if he is promised to someone else?" she asked as much to herself as to Carew.

"Smile, my dear. He is walking this way."

Hope immediately felt very conscious of Rotham's presence and their changed situation. For once, she did not know how to act. It was distinctly uncomfortable to know that his friendship and proximity were no longer hers to command.

Just as he reached them, Hope saw the Duchess watching from across the garden, and that made her spine stiffen. She greeted Rotham with more coolness than she had intended.

"Carew, Miss Whitford," he said with an easy smile. Rotham was looking more dark and dangerous than usual, which only made Hope want him more. But she knew better than to throw herself at his feet. She would not demean herself so—especially in front of the Duchess.

"Lord Rotham." She inclined her head. Should it be a small comfort that he had greeted her before Miss Cunningham?

A waiter walked by with glasses of punch and champagne, and Rotham took one and offered it to her.

"Thank you," she muttered as she accepted it, but could think of nothing else to say.

"Have you heard from Westwood and your sister?"

"Yes, my lord. They have arrived in Paris, and are enjoying the cuisine and shops."

At her side, Carew snorted. "I'll bet."

Hope did not understand the sardonic tone. Perhaps he was more affected than he let on that Faith had chosen Westwood. She sipped on her punch to give her something to do besides talk.

Hope didn't want to hang on Rotham's sleeve—or Carew's, for that matter. She also did not wish to go another Season unwed, which meant she had to make the effort to attract other suitors. All those dreams and fantasies she'd had about having a Season were nothing like the reality. For all she knew, Rotham was as high in the instep as his mother, and had only been doing her a kindness. Had she so wildly mistaken his interest? It did not matter if his marriage to Miss Cunningham was already planned. He certainly had not denied the Duchess' announcement of that fact. She was unaccountably hurt when there was no understanding between Lord Rotham and herself. She had stupidly allowed herself to become infatuated with him, and the only way to cure that was to distance herself.

"Would you excuse me?" She broke away from the gentlemen, needing to be away from him. Whenever Rotham was near, she could think of no one else.

Patience and Grace were still speaking with Miss Cunningham, and Hope made her way towards them. The alternative was to go to the Dowager Lady Westwood, but she was with the Duchess of Davenmere.

Hope stood on the periphery as her sisters and Miss Cunningham were discussing some of their mutual army friends and their Regiment's movement to the country for the summer, causing general woe amongst the eligible misses who relied upon the soldiers for dancing and frivolity.

Hope had drunk her punch too quickly, and excused herself to find the ladies' retiring room, but halted behind a clematis-covered column when she overheard the Duchess talking to Faith's mama-in-law. "They are all passably well-looking, I'll grant you, but I pity you for being taken in, Louisa. They are nothing but commoners looking to better themselves. I would have expected no less from Florence Halbury. Westwood should have sent them right back where they came from with a hired companion to see them suitably placed. To foist them on you to bring out is unforgivable!" Every syllable from her lips dripped with disdain.

"Westwood did so with my blessing, your Grace. Faith is now my daughter, and I could not be more pleased with her. The other girls are equally a delight to me. I enjoy squiring them around immensely."

The Duchess humphed doubtfully. "I suppose there is nothing to be done but keep them away from Rotham."

ENOUGH WAS ENOUGH. Max attended the Cunningham garden party and decided he could not take anything more. He had noticed how Miss Whitford had distanced herself from him every time he'd come near. Curse his mother for ever saying anything about Vivienne!

He had to get away to think, and it seemed as good a time as any to visit his father, the Duke. If he was truly to be cut off, then it was time they came to an understanding. It was hard to imagine his father ever doing such a thing.

It said much about the state of his familial relations that Max rarely went to the ducal seat, but he'd been brought up much like an automaton without love or affection, save from old family retainers such as the nurse and the head groom, with whom he had spent most of his time until he went away to school. Then he'd relished the camaraderie of his friends, whom he was still close to.

His mother had been born and bred to be a duchess, and she thought of nothing but duty and connections. He had seen her twice a year as a child, and even then, he'd only been brought out for her inspection.

His father, on the other hand, was not a stern creature, but allowed himself to be swayed and directed by the Duchess and his steward. He made time for Max when requested, but would much rather be with his hounds and horses than people.

Knowing the Duchess was in London, Max directed his valet to pack for a fortnight in Derbyshire. The ride and distance from the Duchess, and females of marriageable age, would be most welcome.

A long, hard two days' ride eased some of his anger with his mother. City had turned into countryside, then as he'd neared Ashbourne, the gentle climb towards the peaks alleviated the rest.

As he approached Davenmere from the village, he felt detached, even though he'd grown up there and knew it would one day be his. He knew he needed to marry to carry on the ducal line. He might not be attached to the house, but even he had pride in the family name.

As he thought, surveying the pride of the ducal name, he wanted what his mother looked down her aquiline nose at. He wanted to fill the estate with warmth and laughter and affection. A wife. Children. Then he might feel what he ought.

When he thought of who he could share that with, it was not Vivienne Cunningham's innocent blue eyes and angelic face that came to mind. One thing he could say for her was that she was not cold. However, she did not warm his blood as Hope Whitford did—yet would it be fair to Miss Whitford to ask her to be his duchess? It was not an easy task, especially when one had not been brought up to it, and it was a very public position. Max cared little for that, but he could not shield her from it entirely.

But he didn't want to think about marriage at the moment. His mother had put such a distasteful flavour for it into his mouth, and he feared it would throw a dark cloud over any arrangement he wished to make that was not with Vivienne Cunningham. The Duchess had proved her ruthlessness time and time again, and with this latest stunt of trying to announce the betrothal, he feared his ability to properly court anyone else would be doomed to failure.

He urged Romulus forward down the hill to the stables and left the large, bay gelding with the grooms.

"My lord!" Gilford exclaimed with unaccustomed surprise as Max entered the house. "We were not expecting you."

"Am I unwelcome, then?" Max was taken aback.

"Of course not, my lord. I will have everything readied for you."

"Where is my father? I did not see him in the stables or the kennel."

"I believe he is resting in his chambers, my lord."

Max frowned. When had his father ever rested in the afternoon? He turned away and walked towards the stairs that led to the family apartments. He climbed slowly and thoughtfully up the plush burgundy carpets, and past the walls lined with portraits of pompous-looking ancestors wearing their court regalia.

The place was as quiet as a mausoleum, with a distinct lack of warmth. When he reached the end of the upper hallway, and the two large wooden doors with the Davenmere crest intricately carved into the panels, Max decided not to knock. If his father was asleep, he would rather not wake him.

The door swung open quietly to the sitting room and he waited whilst his eyes adjusted to the dim light. It did not smell of soap and beeswax like the rest of the house—it smelled of the sick room. He saw his father's frame, covered in blankets, sitting in an armchair by the fire. What the devil?

Max moved quietly into the room to see if he was asleep.

His generally large, boisterous father looked like a shell of himself. He was thin and frail.

He turned his head and opened his eyes. "Max?" he asked weakly.

"Yes, Father, it is I."

"Thank you for coming. I was afraid you wouldn't read my letter."

Letter? he thought.

"Your mother wanted me to demand you marry the Cunningham chit, of course, but I let her think that was what I wrote." He chuckled softly.

Max kicked himself for not having read the note. "Have you been ill, Father? You have lost several stone."

His father tried to sit upright and began coughing.

Max almost moved to help him, but his father of old would have resented such an action.

Instead, he handed him a glass of water. When the coughing spasm had ceased, he finally spoke.

"That is what I wish to talk to you about. The doctor says I have only a few months to live. Some kind of wasting disease, he says."

Max could not believe what he was hearing. He was still trying to reconcile the body before him as his father's. His once rounded cheeks were hollow and gaunt, and his large girth was thin.

"How long have you known?"

"A couple of months, maybe."

"Does her Grace know?"

"She knew I was ill when she left for London, but she does not know the extent. She was too hell-bent on getting to London to put a stop to your disastrous behaviour, as she put it, to pay me much mind."

"She told me you had cut me off because I refused to wed Miss Cunningham."

His Grace chuckled mildly. "On the contrary, I have called you here to put everything in your hands. Abernathy will answer to you from now on."

"Do you need to tell Diana, Claudia, and Gus? They would want to be here."

His father frowned in thought. "I would much rather them remember me as I was."

"Give them the choice," Max insisted. "Let them decide."

"I will leave that to you," his father said, looking tired. It was hard to believe they were discussing his impending death so rationally.

"So you will support me in allowing me to choose whom I shall marry?"

"My marriage was arranged for me." He looked at Max with a bit of the old twinkle in his eyes. "Yes, I support you making your own choice. I will not be here to see the day, I am afraid."

Max was taken aback that the Duke sounded saddened by the thought. Was it merely his own mortality that made him feel this way now?

"I have always intended to marry one day, but…"

"But your mother sets up your bristles with her meddling," the Duke finished for him.

"Precisely," Max agreed.

"Well, I will not meddle," he said softly as he drifted back to sleep.

"You never have," Max muttered as he stood and left the room quietly, wondering if things would not have been better if he had meddled.

Max went downstairs to find Abernathy to see what the state of his inheritance was. The last thing he had expected to find when he returned was that he would be taking over for his father much, much sooner than he expected. His father had always seemed almost immortal, and Max had not expected to accede to the title for many a long year yet.

He stopped and frowned at the door to the steward's office. Should he marry now? Once he became Duke, it would be much more diffi-cult. Would it be too much for one such as Hope, who had not been bred to such a status? Max hated being rushed or constrained into anything.

Somehow he wanted to do this to please his father, but he knew he could not leave before the Duke's death. He shook his head and rapped once on the door before entering.

"My lord," Abernathy said, as he rose from his chair. "I am glad you came. Your father has not been himself for some time."

"Yes, I have just come from seeing him."

"I urged him to tell you sooner," he said apologetically.

"I do not blame you. He is stubborn. I must confess, however, I did not read the letter. Her Grace presented it to me as an ultimatum, and I did not even open it."

"Yes, I overheard her trying to convince him of the necessity, but whilst your father may have given the appearance of acceding to her wishes, he rarely has."

"Indeed?" Max had always assumed his mother was the backbone behind the dukedom. It was a relief to hear otherwise.

"Here are the papers giving you full control. Once his Grace passes away, things will be made official in Parliament, of course."

Max absently took the papers, which meant very little, as none of it seemed real to him.

"Things are in good order, but there are some urgent matters in need of your attention," the steward said. "Will you be needing to hurry back to London?" he asked.

Max shook his head. "No, Abernathy. I am here for the duration."

CHAPTER 3

*I*t had been a fortnight since Hope had last seen or heard from Lord Rotham. Not that she was counting, but after having seen him every day for months, it was as though he had simply disappeared. The Duchess was still at many of the same entertainments, unfortunately, but not her son.

The Season no longer held the allure it had, and she hated that her enjoyment of the activities seemed to pivot on Rotham's presence.

Why could she not forget about him? She had several perfectly nice, eligible suitors to choose from, and she could not contemplate any of them. Perhaps once Rotham was wed, then she would be able to relinquish hope. But things felt dismal, and if he was never going to be in Society, then she would have no chance of changing his mind.

Most of the matches that had been made that Season were coming to fruition with weddings at Saint George's, Hanover Square, and the rest of the *ton* was making plans to go to the country for various house parties.

"Why the long face?"

Hope turned at Patience's voice. They were all in the upstairs sitting room set aside for their use.

She gave a careless shrug of one shoulder. "I do not know. Perhaps I am weary of the Season."

"When you were the one who was desperate for it?" she argued.

"I would not mind going to a house party or somewhere in the country for the summer," Grace said. "It does not sound like most people remain in Town anyway."

"Has the Dowager mentioned her plans? Or does she mean to spend the summer at Taywards?"

"I have not heard," Grace answered, then they looked at Joy, who always seemed to know everything that was going on from overhearing the servants talk. She did not seem to realize they were all looking at her expectantly.

"Joy?" Grace prompted.

She turned to them. "Oh. I have not heard, either. I miss Faith. When are they expected to return?"

"I do not know," Hope said. She also missed her elder sister's guidance more than she cared to admit. The Dowager was kind, but she did not understand in the same way.

"I miss Westwood and his friends," Patience said frankly. "London is not nearly as much fun without their escort."

"Mr. and Miss Cunningham are still here," Joy said. They had faithfully called upon Joy nearly every day. It still wasn't the same.

"Whatever happened to Lord Rotham?" Grace asked, looking at Hope, who had no idea.

"He went to the country," Joy answered. "He did not tell you?" She looked at Hope.

"Why would he?" she asked a little more forcefully than intended.

"Miss Cunningham says that he avoids her."

"Why would he want to avoid her if she is his intended?" Hope could not help but ask.

"Vivienne says that he does not want to marry her, that it is all their parents' doing."

"And how does she feel about that?" Grace asked.

"She does not seem overly concerned to me," Joy said with an unconcerned shrug as she stroked the cat's back, to his loud purrs in response.

Hope wanted to interrogate Joy further, but she refrained. Her possessiveness of Rotham did her no credit when she had no right to such feelings. "A house party might be just a thing," she said out loud.

"How does one go about being invited to one?" Grace asked.

"We don't go about asking," Patience replied. "We are completely at the mercy of the Dowager's choices."

"She is well connected. Perhaps a hint that such a thing would interest us?" Hope suggested.

"Such a hint would come better from you than me," Grace said. "With many of the officers leaving London, and the Season drawing to a close, there will be little left here to do."

Before, Hope would have had a sharp retort for such an attitude, but she could more than sympathize now.

A servant knocked and entered with a tea tray and some pastries, and Joy immediately perked up. With Westwood and Faith on the Continent, his lordship's chef had delighted in spoiling them with his creations.

"Is there anything on the calendar for this evening?" Hope asked.

"I believe there was a musical evening at Lady Rutherford's or a ball at the Fairmont mansion to celebrate Lady Amelia's betrothal."

"I suppose we are obliged to attend that one, and I do adore Lady Amelia, but I am tired of balls."

"That is normal by the end of the Season," the Dowager said from the doorway. "May I join you?"

"Of course."

"You must try these." Joy held up the remainder of the biscuits that remained for the Dowager to choose from.

She smiled. "I suppose one will not hurt," she said as she selected a chocolate biscuit and took a seat. Hope poured her a cup of tea and added two spoons of sugar before handing it to her.

"I have just received a note that I thought might interest you," she said.

All of them looked up with curiosity. "Is it news from Faith and Westwood?" Patience asked.

"No. I have not heard from them in a couple of days. This is from Davenmere."

"Rotham's father?" Hope asked.

"Davenmere as in the estate," she said. "We have been invited to a house party there."

"From the Duchess?" Hope could not stop the question from escaping her lips. She knew the Duchess did not care for them.

"From Rotham, actually," the Dowager said. "But I have known the Duchess since her first Season. If you do not wish to go, I understand." She gave her a sympathetic, motherly look.

"Do we have any other options?" Patience asked curiously.

"I had only begun to give thought to the matter of what we would do next. As a general rule, I attend a house party and spend part of the summer at Taywards."

"Is Davenmere very grand?" Joy asked.

"It is purported to be the most glorious estate in all of England," the Dowager said. "It is certainly the largest I have been to."

"I remember reading about it in *The Traveller's Guide*," Patience said.

Hope remembered it well. She used to dream about meeting a prince and living in a castle like Davenmere. "Will it be a large party?"

"The invitation does not say, but in the past there have been two or three dozen guests."

Grace gasped.

"The house boasts forty guest chambers," the Dowager remarked.

"It sounds like a palace."

"It is as good as one," the Dowager agreed.

"Oh, please can we go?" Grace asked.

"I am surprised the Duchess would invite us there," Hope said out loud.

"I suspect she was given no choice." The Dowager looked pointedly at Hope with a twinkle in her eyes.

That filled Hope with a glimmer of optimism, but on the other hand, she did not want to be hated by Rotham's mother. She wanted to see his home more than anything, even knowing how hopeless was the whole situation. What was it about human nature that made one torture oneself so?

"Will I be able to bring little Freddy Tiger?" Joy asked.

"I am certain that could be arranged," the now Dowager Viscountess said with a kind smile. "I am sure Rotham will not mind, and if he does, we will simply ask for forgiveness later."

"When will we go?"

"I will send our acceptance now and then we will begin packing. The invitation says as soon as it is convenient."

Hope felt both a mixture of excitement and trepidation. If only she knew who would be there, and what she would be facing.

With the way things had been, she would be forced to watch a formal betrothal announcement and be subjected to all that entailed.

The Dowager left to begin making arrangements.

"Do you think there will be other eligible gentlemen there?" Patience asked.

"I could not begin to say, but I would think Rotham would invite his friends."

"It is too bad their regiment is not to be stationed nearby."

"There could always be another," Joy said with her usual enthusiasm.

"It will not be the same," Patience moaned.

Hope had to agree but didn't say so. Nothing was the same since Faith had married.

MAX CONTEMPLATED NOT TELLING the Duchess about his house party at all, but since he wanted his sisters and brother to come home, it was a necessary evil. When he presented the idea of a house party to his father, the man seemed to brighten at the idea. He'd always loved to invite his friends to hunt and so Max included some of the Duke's friends in the invitations.

After discussing the matter with his Grace, Max and his father decided to send the Duchess a letter describing their terms. Max would invite all of his friends—the Whitford ladies included—and the Duchess was not to mention anything about a betrothal, or be unkind to any of his guests, or she would be sent back to London for the duration. The Duke had even mastered his strength to add his own scribble that Max be left to choose his own bride at the end of the letter. It was the best he could hope for, but he knew his mother could make her disapproval known, even if she kept silent.

He was pleased when the acceptances began to return, and he instructed the servants to have the house prepared as quickly as possible. There was still a week before any of the guests would arrive. He'd heard nothing from his mother, but he had little doubt she would be there.

Cunningham, Carew, and Montford arrived together on the seventh morning after his invitations went out. They found him in the study, amongst dark panelled wood and hunting trophies, rifling through tenant reports.

"What have we here?" Carew asked. "Can it be that hell has frozen?"

"Very funny." Max stood and shook his friends' hands. "I am glad you could come," he said earnestly. His life had certainly changed in a fortnight, from town beau to daily rides around the property, combing through reports, and making monumental decisions about tenants and finances.

"Is it true, then?" Freddy whispered. "The Duke is ill?"

"He said so in his letter, did he not?" Montford chided.

"Unfortunately," Max confirmed. "The doctor has given him only a few months. He has signed all authority over to me. I will not be leaving Davenmere for some considerable time, so we thought to invite everyone here instead."

"So this is the last hurrah?" Montford asked sceptically.

"Of sorts. You know how my father is. Everything is a joke or a laugh."

"I suppose I would not want my last days to be everyone mourning and walking on tiptoe around me either." Freddy would agree, of course.

"Who else is coming?" Carew asked.

"The usual subjects—except Westwood and his bride, of course. I did send them an invitation in Paris, but I have no expectation of them interrupting their wedded bliss."

"Speaking of wedded bliss, how proceeds your matrimonial search?" Freddy asked Monty.

"As a matter of fact, I have dipped my toes into other waters, so to speak."

"Pray tell," Max said, with a guarded look. "It sounds ominous."

"Not ominous, but perhaps scandalous. I do not wish to speak prematurely, but should this work out, there will be no need for me to rush to the altar with an heiress."

"Please tell me you did not cast your lot in with the canal scheme." Max frowned.

"No, but it is a business prospect in the shipping industry. Westwood and Carew have the horse venture, so I thought, why not do something of my own?"

"Do not expect me to be scandalized. More and more of our kind will find themselves in dire straits soon if they do not replenish the monies they are spending," Max said.

"I am grateful to hear your open-mindedness," Montford, the most conservative, traditional of them all, said.

"You thought I would rather see a noose around your neck than you make good investments?" Max shook his head. "I have just been reviewing tenant reports, and whilst they are prosperous, any fool could see that will not be enough for the future. My steward tells me there are rich iron ore deposits on the property that I need to mine."

"If you need investors—" Montford let the suggestion hang.

"I will keep you in mind." He turned to Freddy. "As our properties are adjacent, you are likely to have rich deposits on your own land you could consider mining for yourself."

"I will tell my father," Freddy said.

"I tell you, it's daunting to be responsible for the welfare of so many people."

"I must say I am relieved that you did not call us here for a betrothal announcement. And Viv is much too young," Freddy said.

"Freddy, you know that that was our mothers' wish and nothing more."

"Honestly, that is a relief. No offence to you, Rotham, but when her Grace makes a proclamation, it tends to be the law."

"None taken. Vivienne is more like a sister to me," Max explained.

Freddy nodded his agreement.

"However, and I would prefer this to remain between us, I do intend to marry soon. My father would enjoy seeing me wed, though to the bride of my choice."

Gilford knocked lightly, then brought in a tray with ale and sandwiches. "I thought you might enjoy some refreshment after your travels," he said to the gentlemen, and then bowed his way out.

"Don't mind if I do," Freddy said, and helped himself. "So if not Viv, do you have someone in mind?"

"Miss Hope," Montford answered for Max.

"Oh, I see."

"Freddy, have you been under a rock these past few months?" Montford asked with a shake of his head.

"I am aware they were always paired together, but that does not mean he means to marry her."

"Quite right," Max agreed. "Not everyone is suited to be a duchess, or wants to be one."

Montford scoffed. "I have yet to meet a lady who lacks that ambition."

"The Whitford ladies are lovely, but they were hardly brought up to run grand estates or be political hostesses," Max argued.

"Who cares for that?" Freddy argued. "I'd rather marry someone I liked."

"Hear, hear." Carew raised his ale in a mocking toast.

"You have decided to take an interest in the Lords, then?" Montford always did his duty, and could not let this one pass.

"There are many things that cannot be ignored. I have no inclination to be a great politician, but also I will not shirk my responsibilities there," Max answered.

"I will be glad of a comrade in the House. Carew rarely takes an interest in voting." Montford shot Carew a speaking look.

"Back to the Whitford ladies. They are all intelligent, and could learn what they needed to know. Between your steward, your housekeepers and servants, your estates practically run themselves," Carew pointed out.

"I'd hate to see Miss Hope hurt. It was clear that she was taken with you," Montford added.

Max was instantly offended. "What makes you think I wish to hurt her?"

"Ever since the wedding breakfast, she has looked sad," Carew remarked.

"How is that my fault? I have been here since then."

Carew shrugged. "I assume you have invited eligible ladies here in order to choose your duchess. You and Miss Hope were sitting in each other's pockets until the wedding, at which your mother announced your betrothal to Freddy's sister—which you did not deny, by the by."

"How could I do so without insulting Vivienne?"

"I agree it would have been in poor taste to do so then, but if you did not speak to Miss Whitford—she must assume it to be true."

Max cursed. He hated it when he was wrong and had wronged. He had wanted to go after Hope and explain, but he'd been too furious with his mother to speak to anyone at the time. "She will realize once she arrives. Besides, there was never anything spoken of beyond friendship between the two of us."

All three of his boyhood friends looked at him with disappointment. How did he tell them he was sure that Hope Whitford was his future duchess when he was not certain himself?

"Has it occurred to any of you that Miss Whitford might not wish to marry me?"

They all looked at him blankly.

"No." They answered in unison.

"There will be plenty of time to see who suits. She needs to see exactly what she would be getting. I feel like she only knows part of me—the part of which is not a future duke."

"That may be true," Carew agreed.

Gilford knocked lightly again and entered. "Her Grace has just arrived, my lord, and wishes to speak with you. Are you home?" he enquired.

His friends quickly exited the room. "Cowards!" he called after them. He looked back at Gilford.

Max thought about escaping—bless Gilford for giving him the option—but the rest of the guests could arrive at any time, and his mother would need to understand her place before they did so. "Go ahead and show her in, Gilford. It will be for the best to deal with this now."

"Very good, my lord."

Max could tell his mother was in a fury before she reached him, if the sound of her pumps clicking across the marbled floor was any indication.

He stood and, moving in front of his desk, leaned back against it in a relaxed pose.

The moment she was beyond the threshold, she stopped and narrowed her gaze at him. "What is the meaning of this?"

"Welcome home, your Grace."

"Do not play coy with me!" she fumed.

"Would you care to be more specific?"

"You know perfectly well to what I refer."

"When last we spoke, you scolded me for not attending your house party, so Father and I have decided to host another one. Except this time, we have invited our friends instead of a bunch of schoolroom chits. Why did you not tell me Father was ill?"

"Since when do you care for sniffles and coughs?"

"Since he is dying."

Her head whipped around at that. "I beg your pardon?"

"You heard me correctly. Go and see for yourself, but understand me now. There will be no upsetting him nor any of my guests. I intend for this to be a happy occasion. Is that understood?"

"How dare you speak to your mother in that fashion?" She raised her chin and widened her eyes in affront.

"Believe me, I wish it was not necessary. Had you not issued an ultimatum laced with falsehoods, it would not be necessary. I will choose my own bride, in my own way, and in my own time."

"I suppose I will be forced to endure that Whitford trollop in my own home."

Max was upon her before she took another breath. "That is enough! I will not tolerate another slur against her or her sisters. You may leave now if you are unable to be civil. The Dower House has already been prepared, but you will be forcibly removed from the estate should I hear one more word against her."

She spun about and left the room without another word. Max slumped into a chair, hating that it felt like war against his own flesh and blood. Why did it have to be this way?

CHAPTER 4

Hope had never seen anything more magnificent. She had been too young when her parents died to remember India and then she had been brought up in Bath. Bath was beautiful in its own right, with its golden stone and Georgian façades, but seeing it every day made it lose some of its allure.

Davenmere was another species altogether. Her sisters and the Dowager had driven through the countryside for hours, and then suddenly there it was, nestled in the side a hill as if suspended above its surroundings.

It was a large, three-sided manse in the Baroque style, built with limestone native to Derbyshire. A lake stood before the house, bearing a fountain shooting upwards of twenty feet in the air, while one of the peaks of the district and thick woods provided the remainder of the setting.

They could see it long before they entered the gates, and even then, they drove through the woods and across a river over a beautiful stone bridge before they finally reached the house. A harmonious blend of carefully designed gardens, idyllic countryside, and the untamed beauty of the peaks all contributed to the grandeur.

Her sisters were exclaiming about the palace—for there really was no other way to describe it—but Hope kept silent. There was too much to take in for her to speak about it. And she had thought herself a good match for Rotham? What a little fool she'd been!

When the carriage rolled up before the house, there were grooms and footmen, and a whole host of servants in their smart, matching blue and gold livery, waiting for them.

Hope was the last to alight from their carriage, and she took a deep breath, trying to steal her nerves to indifference. It was only a house. He was only a man. She had to learn to be at peace with that.

Pushing herself forward off the seat, she was surprised to see a hand extended out to her.

Rotham himself was waiting to hand her out.

"Rotham," she said breathlessly, cursing his effect on her. So much for indifference.

Many gentlemen were handsome, but his dark eyes and lean build caused a reaction similar to tinder smouldering before the spark of fire.

"Welcome to Davenmere, Miss Whitford."

Hope did not like the change in her name since Faith had married. It sounded too formal on his lips.

Hope looked at his extended hand, which was still awaiting her grasp, and took it, ignoring the warmth she felt at his touch. She looked around once her feet were on the ground and realized the others had already gone inside. Had she tarried so long that Rotham had come looking for her?

"I am glad you came. Forgive me for being unable to say a proper farewell in London. My father is not well and desired for me to come to him."

"I am sorry to hear it. I hope he is on the mend. Are you certain we will not disturb him?" she asked as they gained the steps to the house.

"Unfortunately, he is not expected to recover, but he is in good spirits and loves to have people around him."

Hope did not know how to respond. He seemed quite casual about the situation, but she supposed he could hardly behave otherwise.

"I beg you to make yourself at home and avail yourself of the gardens, the stables, and anything else you wish."

"Thank you, my lord."

Hope tried not to gawp as she took in the opulence of the entrance hall. Her eyes were immediately drawn to the ceiling, which was covered in a mural of boldly coloured renaissance art of goddesses dancing in moonlight. The black and white marble floor was accentuated with statues of what, to her untrained eye, were Roman, or perhaps Greek relics.

"One of my ancestors was rather obsessed with Roman antiquities. He found a mosaic on the estate, which is now surrounded by a bath house to give it its proper setting. Then he decided the entire house needed to be a shrine to those who came before," Rotham said, his voice laced with amusement.

"A real Roman mosaic?"

"I will show it to you sometime. I can only be thankful that they chose some of the less outrageous Roman names to add to our heritage."

"Dare I ask what your siblings' names are?"

"My full name is Maximus, my elder sister is Diana, my younger sister is Claudia, and my younger brother is Augustus."

"Those are not too outrageous," she agreed.

"Had it been my father who was the antiquarian, the names would have been more interesting."

Hope laughed. "I look forward to meeting him." The old ease was there, and it almost made things worse. Part of her had feared she might be ignored.

At that moment, the housekeeper came down the stairs. She was dressed in severe black wool, with her silver hair pulled back into a cap and a ring of keys dangling at her waist.

"Here is Mrs. Watson returning from showing the Dowager and your sisters upstairs. You would probably like to join them to refresh yourself. I believe there will be a light repast on the back terrace at four."

Hope didn't want this time alone with him to end, but there was little she could say that would not make her look ridiculous.

"My lord," Hope said in farewell.

The housekeeper bobbed a curtsy to Hope. "Your chambers are ready, Miss Whitford. Shall I take you to them?"

Hope instantly felt insecure with this woman. She might be a servant, but she had served a duke and duchess for most of her life, Hope assumed. Was this her normal demeanour or had the Duchess poisoned the servants against her? Hope scolded herself. Very likely the Duchess thought Hope so far beneath her that she had not given her a second thought. Many servants of grand houses thought they were superior. That was probably all it was. The housekeeper at Halbury had been so kind and loving to them that she had assumed all country housekeepers were the same.

Hope followed the woman up the grand staircase, then beyond several large drawing rooms, a music room, and what looked to be a library. They turned down a hallway that overlooked a courtyard, and then another hallway before embarking on another set of stairs to a different wing. Hope tried to remember landmarks so she did not become lost. When they stopped before a pair of large, panelled doors with butterflies carved upon them, the housekeeper took out her keys and unlocked them.

Hope was expecting her sisters to be sharing a room with her, but no one was there. The door opened into a bright chamber of soft jonquil and cream with embroidered butterflies on the coverlet and wallpaper.

"Where are my sisters?" Hope asked.

"They are on the same passage, but his lordship specifically wanted you in this room." Her face was so stoic that Hope could not tell whether she approved or disapproved.

"Will you be needing anything else for now?" she asked.

"No, thank you, Mrs. Watson," Hope said in dismissal.

There was warm water on the wash-stand and a fresh cake of soap that smelled of almonds and honey. She splashed her face and washed her hands, and then walked over to a set of French doors which had been left open to let in the summer breeze. They led out to a small balcony, from which the view could only be described as picturesque.

As the house was nestled into the side of a peak, before her was a cliff face which boasted a small waterfall that ran down into the river which they had crossed earlier. The view then extended out over a meadow dotted with grazing sheep.

Knowing Rotham had selected it just for her made her feel special, though it was probably more to do with the fact that she usually wore jonquil than anything else. She was dwelling too much on it. No doubt all the chambers in a duke's mansion were equally grand.

There was nothing left for her to do but find her sisters. The hall held at least a dozen chambers, and she wished she had asked specifically which ones her sisters occupied. However, as she progressed, she was able to hear their voices. They had been placed in a large chamber with two beds.

"There you are, Hope. We were wondering what had become of you!" Grace said.

"I was speaking with Lord Rotham and was left behind."

Patience turned and smiled knowingly at her, which Hope chose to ignore.

"Where is Joy?"

"She went with Mr. Cunningham. Apparently, there is a new litter of puppies."

"Where is her chamber?"

Grace smiled. "Through here."

Hope had missed a door that was connected behind the screen. Behind it was a smaller but enchanting room that was circular with floor-to-ceiling windows. It was fanciful and fairy-like and perfect for Joy. Hope walked to the window and looked out to a view of horses in the meadow in the distance, feeling that perhaps everything was going to work out. How indifferent could he be if he had taken such care to select rooms for her sisters and herself?

Max watched Miss Whitford go upstairs with the housekeeper and reminded himself to be careful. Their friendship made being with her natural, but it still did not mean she was the best choice for his duchess. He had seen the look Mrs. Watson had given her, and by favouring her with one of the best chambers, he had already signalled to his household that he had a preference for Miss Whitford.

In order to make the best decision, he had asked several young ladies to visit and vowed to give them all fair consideration. He'd even asked Vivienne Cunningham to attend, because it would look poorly not to include her, and he wanted to make certain he wasn't excluding her because of his mother's preference.

However, there were enough eligible bachelors there that Vivienne could very well choose someone else.

"Max!" Diana said and greeted him. Max adored all his siblings, but Diana was closest to him in age and looks, except she was softer in demeanour, and wore the glow of motherhood like a badge of honour.

"You came! When did you sneak in?"

"Of course I came! We have only just arrived. How could I ignore what you said about Father? I have not seen him yet."

"Prepare yourself. I had no warning myself and received quite a shock."

"Mother did not tell you he was ill?"

"I do not think she had any notion of it herself."

"Why the house party, Max? Would it not have been better to share this in private as a family?"

"I debated it, but then Father mentioned he would like to see me wed, and you know how he thrives with people around him."

Max almost laughed at the look on his sister's face.

"Please do not tell her Grace my intentions. We have already had a falling out over Miss Cunningham."

"That child? She is almost of an age with my Susan."

"Indeed. I always say she is much like a sister, but the reality is, she is more like my niece."

"Do you have someone in mind? I assume the ladies you have invited are the candidates?"

"Not all of them, but some, yes."

She eyed him a little too knowingly. "Do you have one in particular in mind? I assume this is what I get for living in Northumberland? I know none of what has been happening in London!"

"If you were a better correspondent, I am certain someone would enlighten you. Instead, you have been breeding an entire cricket team."

Diana laughed. "There are only six of them, Max. And I am a passable correspondent, but so much of what my friends tell me is gossip, of which not even half is true."

"You were aware that Westwood married, I assume?"

"The catch of the Season, yes. To some previously unknown provincial girl he had been named guardian of."

"Faith Whitford," Max supplied. "She happens to have four sisters, and when a situation arose where they needed protection, Westwood asked me and our friends to help."

"So one of them has taken your fancy?" Diana grinned.

"She is lovely, yes, but I do not think she has any idea of what being a duchess would mean, nor has she been bred to it."

"So by bringing her here, do you mean to test her?" Diana looked disbelieving.

"I mean to let her see if it is something she would want, while at the same time also seeing if any of the other ladies might suit."

"I think you are playing with fire, Max. If word gets out…"

He held up his hand. "Word will not get out. Mother tried to force my hand in London, and therefore I am being extremely cautious. We had a grand row over it, and I have made it clear she is not to interfere. However, I will need you to play hostess."

Diane looked sideways at him. "I expect you to give me more detail than that."

"Later. Guests are arriving."

"Very well. I will play hostess, but I mean to enjoy every minute."

The remainder of the afternoon was spent greeting arrivals, and thankfully, his sister played her part beautifully.

Even though the Cunninghams were their neighbours, there were still several miles to travel between the two estates, so they would be staying at Davenmere.

Lord Brosner had an eligible sister, so they also numbered amongst the guests.

Unfortunately, Max had felt obliged to invite Lady Wilton and her two daughters. The eldest, Lady Agatha, was not too much of an antidote—an accolade everyone wished for in a future bride.

Montford's mother, Lady Conway, and sister, Lady Caroline, also arrived, bringing equal numbers of eligible gentlemen and ladies. Max scoffed at his thoughtfulness. The remainder of the guests were composed of older friends of the Duke and Duchess of Davenmere. Hopefully, it looked like an ordinary house party.

Max had not yet heard whether the Duchess had chosen to sulk in her apartments or remove to the Dower House. She had not been seen since her arrival. He did not dare hope that she had returned to London.

His friends had retired to the billiards room with most of the other men. Before he greeted them, he turned when he heard his father's familiar, boisterous laugh. Max could only smile. He was happy if the old fellow felt well enough to leave his chambers. It seemed like he had improved a bit with his friends present.

Max saluted his father, who was surrounded by his old cronies, then wandered over to Montford and Carew, who were playing against one another.

Max dropped into the leather chair next to Freddy and crossed his legs as one of his footmen placed a decanter of brandy with glasses on the table between them.

"Your father looks pleased," Freddy remarked. "I almost would not know he was ill, had he not dropped five stone."

"His spirits have certainly improved with his friends being here. Hopefully, it will not overtax him."

Freddy laughed. "He was just discussing bringing out the hounds for a hunt since the ground is soft enough from the recent rains."

"Was he?" Max asked. "I suppose I should not be surprised. If I were at the end, I would do all the things that brought me joy. I shall see that it happens if that is his wish."

Carew struck a perfect strike and curved the black, potting it into the pocket for the win. He smiled with satisfaction.

"That was devilish clever, Carew," Montford said, appreciatively conceding the win.

"Are you certain you wish to fulfil all your father's wishes?" Carew asked Max perceptively as he leaned on his cue.

Max poured four glasses of brandy and handed them around.

"Of course, I will not commit to something I am not certain of," he answered casually.

"I am glad to hear it. I have seen too many comrades fall on the sword of familial duty."

"I am acutely aware of it."

"And I would hate for anyone's hopes to be raised."

Had he deliberately put emphasis on the word hope? "As would I," Max drawled. "It is why I am not mentioning my intentions to anyone."

"I wonder if Westwood is having any regrets yet?" Freddy asked.

"That was a perfect match if ever I've seen one. Nothing less would have served for Westwood," Montford retorted.

"Let us be honest, there are not many ladies in the *ton* like the Whitford sisters," Carew remarked.

"Their beauty is incomparable," Rotham agreed.

"I am not talking about their beauty. I would not want someone for them who only valued that."

This was getting out of hand, but Max would not commit himself to anyone yet. Max did not know what Carew was about. Did he want Hope for himself or to bring Max to heel? He was such a staunch defender of the ladies, but he had always had a face for cards and kept his true intentions to himself.

"Would you care for a game?" Max asked.

"Always," Carew said and pushed away from the table.

CHAPTER 5

*H*ope was joined in Joy's chamber by Grace and Patience. Both of them gasped when they saw it. "I had no idea this existed. It is magical!"

"It suits Joy perfectly."

"Oh, I could live here forever." Grace sighed dreamily.

"Only dukes and kings live this way," Patience replied in her usual pragmatic fashion.

"I am quite certain that marquesses and earls often have similar estates. Even Taywards is magnificent."

"Regardless of that, one of our sisters has already defied the odds to marry a lord. I do not think that luck will hold for all of us."

Hope swallowed hard. Patience was right. She should not even allow herself to daydream about such things.

"Are you sad about Rotham and Miss Cunningham?" Grace asked. "I had thought…"

Hope shook her head. "A girlish fantasy is all it was. I have learned my lesson. I feel sorry for him, but he cannot marry as he wishes."

"I do not know why a dowry matters so much to someone with all this." She waved her hand around at the magnificence.

"Miss Cunningham does not even hold a title," Patience pointed out. Thankfully, Joy was not present or she would have defended Freddy's name somehow.

"But it is an old and respected name," Hope pointed out. "Not that there is anything to tarnish ours, but our parents were poor missionaries. We only have the dowry we do because of Lady Halbury."

"Saving souls should be more respected than some stupid family name." Grace sounded very young and very much like Joy at that moment. Hope tended to agree, but it was not the way Society worked.

"Why do you think we were really invited here?" she found herself asking.

"I heard the Dowager saying to her maid, Jenkins, that there had not been a house party here in almost a decade. It is a bit suspicious, do you not think? And Rotham was the one to put it into place?"

"Really? I suppose I did hear her saying he sent the invitation. Why is that, do you think?"

"I do not know if this is true or not." Patience leaned forward and spoke quietly. "But the maid also said she heard his Grace was ill and that he told Lord Rotham he had to marry before he died."

Hope covered the involuntary squeak that came from her mouth.

Patience continued. "My theory is that he brought us all here to choose a wife."

"But he is already betrothed to Vivienne Cunningham," Hope said miserably.

"That is what the Duchess wants everyone to think."

It was what Rotham had also said to her, but still, Hope did not know how to fight against the blessing of the Duchess. She didn't even want to think about how intimidating the Duke would be.

"I think you are the one he really wants," Patience said.

"It doesn't matter what he wants," Hope argued. "He will be a duke, and to the *ton*, we are the daughters of poor missionary folk."

"Not just folk, but a gentleman and a lady," Grace chimed in. "And now our sister is a viscountess. And we have the sponsorship of one."

"You truly think that it is why we are here?"

"I do," Patience nodded.

The thought that she still had a chance bubbled warmth inside Hope like champagne.

"And we will help," Patience said as if reading her thoughts.

"I am afraid to ask what you mean to do," Hope replied warily.

"We can be extra eyes and ears." She ticked off on two of her fingers. "We can make excuses for you should you find yourself able to catch a few moments alone with him, and we can also interrupt or be a nuisance if another lady is hoarding him."

"Hoarding him?"

"Yes, as in monopolizing him. Jenkins told me that the servants become spies during these house parties in order to gain advantages such as time alone with desired persons."

Hope looked at her sister in horror. "I had no idea you and Jenkins had become so close."

Patience waved a dismissive hand in the air. "I am naturally observant and therefore hear things that many do not. It is a feather in the cap of a servant to work for the highest-ranking peer. There is an entire hierarchy below stairs that is even more pronounced at gatherings such as this."

"Fascinating," Grace said.

"I suppose I know something of that, but Halbury was small and everyone seemed to rub along so well."

"I miss Halbury," Grace said with sadness, having just said she wanted to stay there forever. "Everything was so much simpler."

"That is the truth. I would never have thought I would need to bribe servants to have a chance for happiness."

"Kindness goes a long way," Patience added. "Whilst the servants here are loyal to Davenmere, they prefer Lord Rotham to the Duchess, which is only natural considering her disposition and his being the next duke."

Hope shook her head. "I do not want to know how you learned that so quickly."

Patience laughed and Hope and Grace joined in. It felt good to be silly again.

"In all seriousness, Hope, I do think you need to plan out your campaign. Certainly, the other ladies and their mamas are doing so," Patience advised.

"You make it sound like a battle! Too much time with your army court, I have no doubt. But I have the advantage of being friends with him."

Patience shook her head. "That will only go so far at a house party. Yes, the country is more relaxed than Town, but there are still planned activities where the gentlemen are together most of the day, and the ladies have their own amusements. In the evenings, there will be dinners and balls or games."

"I am afraid to ask, but what do you think I should do?"

"I can tell you what I think. I think he wants to see your suitability to be a duchess, which is not at all the same thing as being his wife."

Hope's excitement was short-lived. Her spirits sank. "Do you mean I have to behave like his mother?"

"No, silly. Just show that you could play hostess or manage the household."

"I can hardly push myself forward in such a vulgar fashion! His sister is his hostess, and he has a perfectly formidable housekeeper!"

Patience laughed. "That is not what I meant. Perhaps just showing understanding of the little things will be enough."

"You mean that we are the last to go in to dine at every meal?" Hope asked rhetorically with no end of sarcasm.

"Well, yes. That is what I mean."

"I refuse to put on airs. I think that would be worse—and have them all gossip about me as though I'm above myself."

"No, you wouldn't want to do that," Grace agreed.

"Just be mindful of it. And I could be wrong, but from Rotham's perspective, he might wonder if you'd even want him, knowing what came with it."

"I doubt he has even thought about it. It is so natural to him, he must think everyone lives like this," Grace said.

"I am certain the Duchess has pointed out my many flaws and unsuitability," Hope added.

There was a knock on the door and their maid entered. "The

Dowager sent me to help you change," she said. "Jenkins is waiting to help you, Miss Hope."

"Is it so late already?" Hope asked.

"It is three o'clock, miss," she answered.

"I just want to stay in this room forever," said Grace, who was the most introverted of the three, with a heavy sigh.

"My room also has a lovely view," Hope said with understanding.

"I am certain the other guests will be all that is delightful," Patience said reassuringly as if she understood their hesitation. "Just think about one thing at a time. Tea on the terrace is not so daunting, is it?"

Hope went to her room, where Jenkins had already laid out a dainty jonquil muslin for the afternoon. She wondered if the maid had even realized she was matching the bedchamber.

Once Hope was dressed, Jenkins styled her hair with soft curls wound with a matching ribbon at the nape of her neck.

After Jenkins had left her, she stood at the balcony looking out, contemplating her next move. She'd never been one for scheming and did not want to have to sink to such measures, but if she wanted Rotham, would she have to fight for him? How easy had things been between them before that she had taken for granted!

Suddenly, she was a bundle of nerves, feeling as though she'd have to put on a performance. Hope wanted to be herself, but perhaps that was the point. Was being a duchess presenting two faces to the world?

As long as you can be with Rotham, her conscience whispered.

Would he be different as duke? She had often seen a softer side to him when they'd been amongst only friends. Perhaps that was the price she'd have to pay. It was definitely something she needed to consider while she still had the chance. If only they could just be Hope and Max, she did not need anything else but him.

Hope turned when she heard a noise. She looked around and saw that a piece of paper had been slipped beneath her door.

She hurried over and picked it up, burning with curiosity as to who would be sneaking about leaving notes. She opened the door, but could see or hear nothing but an empty corridor. She unfolded the paper and read out loud.

I WILL BE WATCHING YOU.

ROTHAM? she wondered at first. But if it was from him, why would it be secretive? It felt more like a threat.

MAX TRIED NOT to seek out Miss Whitford with his eyes, but he knew the moment she and her sisters arrived outside. Deliberately, he forced himself to keep his eyes away from Miss Hope.

Everyone was mingling on the terrace on this late summer's eve. Tables were laid out with light foods from sandwiches and fruit to pastries and ices. Meanwhile, tea, lemonade, and punch were being handed out by the footmen.

All of the players in the act were finally present, but he had to force himself to look at the other ladies. He had not yet formulated a plan on how to speak to and interview the ladies, as it were. In looks, Vivienne Cunningham was the only one who was comparable, even though she was the opposite of Miss Whitford.

Lady Caroline was pleasant and a little older than the others, which made for conversation above the average. She had the same auburn hair as her brother and was built much like him.

Brosner's sister, Lady Alice, was probably his second favourite choice, however, because she was a devout bluestocking and had never pursued him as most of the others or their mothers had done. He and Brosner had never been close, but their fathers and mothers had been good friends. As the daughter of a marquess, Lady Alice would know perfectly how to manage the responsibilities of a duchess. They were late arrivals, so he had not yet spoken more than a greeting to them.

"Brosner, Lady Alice, I trust your chambers are satisfactory?" He took the opportunity to make a brief mental survey of the lady's assets. She had thick brown hair and intelligent hazel eyes. She was not traditionally pretty, but he would consider her handsome.

"Rotham." Brosner shook the hand that was held out to him while Lady Alice inclined her head. "Everything is lovely, my lord. Thank you for inviting us."

"London was interminably dull," Brosner drawled.

"How can you say so?" Lady Alice scolded. "Museums, theatre, and reading salons—I could spend all day, every day, and never see or read everything London has to offer."

"I am afraid you may find Davenmere very slow, my lady, but perhaps some of the tomes in my father's library will meet with your satisfaction. Please help yourself."

"Thank you, my lord."

"I heard a rumour there will be hunting," Brosner said hopefully, as one who was always searching for sport.

"I have heard the same," Max confirmed. "My father will do anything to show off his hounds. It is not the right time of year for it, of course, but we will humour his Grace by taking out the hounds and chasing them across the fields."

"What a vile set of murderers the male species is!" Lady Alice said with open disgust.

"Alice," Brosner growled. "We have discussed this."

"You have told me to keep my mouth closed, you mean. What kind of person would I be if I did not speak what I know to be right?"

"Why do you care about vermin?" Brosner asked.

"I care about all of God's creatures, Ned."

Max was acutely uncomfortable, but could hardly excuse himself politely in the middle of their argument. It was not one he cared to be drawn in to.

"What do you think, Lord Rotham?"

He thought he had already crossed her off his list, was what. He did not mind her having her own opinions, but rather minded the lack of diplomacy about how she expressed them.

"Do you not eat meat, Lady Alice?"

"I do not," she said with her nose in the air and eyes narrowed in challenge.

"I commend your dedication to your beliefs. I, however, am a hunter and carnivore. I see my sister trying to draw my attention. Will you excuse me?" He beat a hasty retreat away from the siblings before it escalated any further.

Max was already tired of this game and felt he'd done enough for one day. In fact, he had already eliminated one possibility. He found Carew, Montford, and Freddy and waved to one of the footmen to bring them drinks.

"Just think, it would be much worse in London," Carew said, not hiding his amusement.

"True, except here there is no escape."

"Thankfully, there is no ultimatum, simply something I am considering to please my father. I am not a martyr, however." He selected a glass of punch from the footman.

"To me, the choice is obvious."

Max followed Carew's gaze to where Hope Whitford was laughing with—his father? He jerked his head back because he had been staring. His friends were also laughing—at him.

"As always, I am delighted to provide your entertainment."

"What is your hesitation?" Freddy asked. "You do not need to marry an heiress and Miss Hope is a great gun." That was the highest compliment Freddy could pay anyone.

"I have my reasons. Besides, it takes more than being a 'great gun' to be a duchess."

"Does that really matter? Are you looking for a replica of your mother?" Carew asked, rather too perceptively.

"You know that is the last thing I want."

"Good, because some of your father's friends look rather interested in Miss Whitford for themselves."

Max did not doubt any of the men there would be interested in one such as Hope.

"Wasn't Summerton looking for a younger wife?" Montford asked.

Max scowled. "He is. He is still hoping to find a young wife to give him an heir."

"It might be a good match, then—if you do not want her, of course. She would be a rich widow before too long."

Max held up his hand. "Enough, all of you. I have my reasons for doing things this way."

"Come now, you cannot blame us for being curious about certain reasons," Freddy said. "Especially when you invite the likes of Lady Wilton's chits and Lady Alice."

Fair point. He was now wondering what had come over him as well. He would have to endure a fortnight with all of them for his sins. "Frankly, I could not think of any other eligible ladies."

His friends looked at him with a mixture of pity and shock.

"I thought I should look at each of them objectively to make certain I made the right choice."

"He must be feverish," Freddy said, looking at him with concern.

"You've had years to assess who is available, Rotham," Montford said with a shake of his head.

The Duke's laughter rumbled loudly, and Max could not help but steal a glance. Hope was the loveliest female he had ever laid eyes upon. And she was a great gun. He could not imagine his mother ever being described as such, but was that a good thing? What did he want in his wife and duchess?

Carew let out a low whistle.

Max turned to see what had elicited such a response.

With a poisonous gleam in her eye, the Duchess was heading straight for where the Duke was speaking with Miss Hope.

Max's blood began to simmer. He had warned her not to interfere. He forced himself to wait and see what his father would do, but did not think the Duke would tolerate the Duchess being rude to an invited guest.

He wanted to go to Hope and avert any embarrassment, but he knew he could not. He watched, waiting for the disaster to unfold.

"You will break that glass if you do not relax," Carew said, and Max deliberately eased his grip and strained to hear what passed between his parents.

As expected, the Duchess completely ignored Hope and spoke directly to the Duke. "Davenmere, do you not think it time you rested?"

"Why ever would I do that when I have such pleasant company? I can rot in my room as well as I can sitting here on the terrace."

Really, what did his mother intend to accomplish by confronting him in such a manner? For all she'd preached propriety and decorum, she was only making herself look ridiculous. Hopefully, she would not embarrass Hope.

"I was just speaking with old Chappy Whitford's daughter here."

"I do not recall such a person," she said stiffly.

"Of course you have heard me speak of him. He was the Navy chaplain who nursed me back to health after Cadiz." He turned to his friends. "Before I became Davenmere, you understand. We served under Nelson together, God rest his soul."

Could it be true? His father had known Hope's? Or was his father more canny than Max had ever realized? Either way, the Duchess could hardly ignore Miss Whitford now.

"It is a shame your parents were killed, Miss Whitford. A finer man I have yet to know," his father continued.

"Thank you, your Grace," Miss Whitford replied as his mother sniffed and left in a huff.

CHAPTER 6

Dinner that evening was a grand affair. Hope wondered if they intended to have formal dinners every night of the house party. It was hard to imagine the servants preparing such lavish feasts night after night.

Jenkins had been sent to help Hope dress and had laid out a lavender silk that was rather daring. She had thought that one had been made for a ball.

"The Dowager asked me to have you wear this one in particular, miss."

Hope thought all of her new clothes were beautiful and had no particular opinion one way or the other. "If her ladyship thinks I should wear this gown, then that is what I shall wear."

The maid looked relieved. Did she think Hope would be difficult?

Jenkins seemed to take extra care with Hope's coiffure, curling and pinning every lock just so. Then she piled all of the curls on top of Hope's head with a few pieces cascading down to her shoulders. Hope had never felt so sophisticated in all her life. Lady Halbury would probably have had a fit at the low cut of Hope's gown, were she able to see her. Part of her shoulders and a good deal of her neck were bare. She rather liked the effect.

"Would you like the pearls, miss?" Jenkins asked, holding them up for her.

Hope looked at her reflection in the mirror. "I think just my locket." It was the one thing each of them possessed from their parents. It was a gold heart with her initials upon it, hanging on a simple gold chain.

She put on her slippers and her gloves and then went down the hall to find her sisters. When they reached the drawing room where everyone was gathered beforehand, Lady Diana was telling them who would escort them into the dining room.

"Good evening, ladies," she said to the Dowager and the sisters. She looked down at her list, then up to search for the desired escorts. "Your escort will be Lord Summerton, my lady," she said to the Dowager. "Miss Whitford..." She frowned. "That's odd, I could have sworn you were paired with someone else," she murmured. "Mr. Cunningham will be your escort. You are acquainted with him?"

"Oh, yes. I know him well."

"Excellent." She pointed out Montford for Patience, and Lord Carew for Grace. At least they had not been paired with any old men, but she did notice Lord Rotham had been paired with Vivienne Cunningham. That was no surprise, if the Duchess was making the arrangements.

What she would not give to see the list Lady Diana had been holding close to her bodice of midnight-blue silk dotted with tiny diamonds. It was clear her original partner had been changed. It mattered not. Freddy was always delightful.

When they went into the dining room, their placement at a separate table was also obvious. It was customary to be seated by rank, or favour of the presiding host, but the three sisters did not even rank high enough to be seated at the main table. A smaller one had been added just for them.

"Please accept our apologies, gentlemen, since you have been relegated to the low-ranking table," Hope teased.

"This is the best table by far," Carew said. "Now I do not have to be subjected to Lady Wilton's wandering hands beneath the table or Summerton's odiferous breath."

"Besides, we are served earlier here," Freddy said knowingly.

"It is the same food," Montford added.

"And we can talk across the table," Patience said.

"I am fairly certain we are still supposed to observe proper etiquette," Hope replied dryly.

"Why bother when 'tis just ourselves?"

"Indeed. We can gossip our hearts out," Carew drawled. "Who should we start with?" he asked as a footman placed bowls of white soup before them.

"I will go first." Patience leaned forward with a twinkle in her eyes. "My maid said one of the young ladies in attendance has found herself in an interesting condition, and must find someone to marry her before the house party ends."

All three of the gentlemen stopped eating and looked up with pale faces.

"You must find out who it is," Carew commanded in the harshest voice Hope had ever heard him speak.

"You do realize we are all eligible bachelors, and therefore targets?" Montford added.

"I had not thought about that." Patience frowned.

"We must never be alone. Our rooms are next to each other's, so we must go everywhere together," Montford said, looking between the other gentlemen.

"As I assume this lady in an interesting condition is not any of you, I must agree. Perhaps your sister would not be so bad, Cunningham, but I rather prefer to choose my own wife and father my own child when the time comes," Carew drawled.

"I cannot believe a lady would try to trick someone like that!" Grace said with all the righteous indignation of an innocent maiden.

"It happens quite often," Freddy assured her. "Half the *ton* have other people's brats foisted upon them. However, I feel the need to point out that such a discussion is not a matter for the dinner table and I stand in great danger of being put off my soup."

Hope shook her head as her sisters blushed and looked at their laps.

"It is too shocking to contemplate. Patience, you should be ashamed of yourself for repeating such tittle-tattle."

Suitably chastened, they all turned their attentions to their soup.

"I do not like thinking the worst of people." Hope frowned, unable to let the situation go. Unconsciously, they all turned their gazes towards the main table and the other possibilities.

"You must learn to overcome that," Carew warned. He paused for a moment before adding, in a bracing tone, "Besides, you would not want some poor fellow trapped, would you now?"

"Poor fellow?" Montford mocked. "Though no one is deserving of that," he added quickly.

"My money is on one of the Wilton chits," Freddy said, forgetting his earlier objections.

"Why is that?" Patience added.

"Because, to be frank, I cannot imagine anyone…"

Carew coughed loudly.

"I cannot imagine my sister, either," Montford agreed.

"Besides, they are always trying to entrap some unwary fool," Freddy continued. "I cannot understand why Rotham invited them here."

"Their father is a chum of the Duke," Montford explained.

"I promise to rescue you if I see any of you alone," Grace assured the gentlemen.

"You're a good girl," Carew said with a brotherly smile.

Oh, dear. That was not at all how Grace wanted him to look at her. Hope felt sad for her sister. "It could be just a malicious rumour," Hope felt compelled to say.

"It could," Montfort agreed. "Lesser rumours have been known to be spread by mamas hoping to give their own daughters an advantage."

"I had no notion the *ton* would be so ruthless," Patience remarked.

"Oh, yes. Rotham's worst enemy is his own mother. Remember

when you and your sister found us at Westwood's hunting box?" Freddy asked Hope.

"Yes, of course."

"Rotham had been set up at a house party arranged by his mother. He barely escaped in time."

"He left the party?"

"Before it really started. The Duchess was furious."

"'Tis a wonder, then, that he decided to host this one," Patience remarked.

"I agree. I believe it was for his father," Montford said quietly. "Poor Rotham has had so many lures thrown out to him. I do not envy his plight."

"Frankly, I am surprised he does not wed someone just to stop the nonsense," Carew added.

"That is exactly what the Duchess wants and therefore why he has refused so far. I do not blame him. I would not want to marry just anyone either," Freddy said.

Hope listened, feeling ill. Had she known, she would have guarded her heart more closely.

They quieted as the soup was removed, and several dishes, such as John Dory fish in a creamy mushroom sauce, salmon with lemon and capers, and roasted partridge wrapped in bacon, were placed around the table for them to serve themselves. Hope wanted none of them, though she selected one and made a small effort.

Something occurred at the head table, causing everyone sitting there to laugh. Hope tried not to feel left out.

"I agree that Rotham threw this house party for his father. Perhaps the Duke begged him to choose a bride before, you know..." Patience stated as though the conclusion were obvious.

Hope noticed the looks that passed between the gentlemen. Was Patience right?

Suddenly, the fish in her mouth tasted like ash. She hated the thought that she only had a short time to prove herself. That made everything even worse.

~

HER GRACE THOUGHT she was so clever, Max fumed inwardly. She had rearranged the seating plan to make certain he was sitting next to Vivienne Cunningham and as far from Hope Whitford as possible. The Duchess might not have full power, but she was determined to put a spoke in his wheel however she could. Next time, he would warn Diana and the servants not to let her Grace make changes. Max had left the seating to Diana, because he didn't want subconsciously to favour Miss Whitford. However, he knew Diana would not have paired him with Vivienne. It would serve her right if he sent her back to London for the slight she'd served the Whitford ladies that night.

Part of the problem with Miss Cunningham was that she agreed with everything Max said and would giggle the rest of the time. Truly, she would be better served to stay in the schoolroom with Susan and Joy until she had matured a little, being only a few months beyond them in age.

Max looked at the other table with longing. They were talking and laughing openly like old friends do. He dragged his gaze back to the main table and muttered something to his other dinner partner that really required little participation from him. Summerton was in the midst of one of his monologues on the new corn laws. Lady Alice objected to something Summerton said, and they began a belligerent discussion usually reserved for gentlemen within the confines of a club. Why was it again that he did not think Hope qualified? He would try to ascertain how she felt about things when next he had the chance, but his mind was made up in one respect. Lady Alice, with her opinionated disposition, was definitely not compatible.

Vivienne was speaking with Lord Wilton, so Max took the opportunity to survey the other ladies on his list.

He turned to see Lady Matilda watching him with a predatory look. He raised an eyebrow at her, letting her know he saw her watching. He had never really given her much consideration since she was younger than Lady Agatha, but there was definitely something about her that was uncomfortable. He had seen that look before in determined mamas…and card sharps.

With a coy glance, she began to mouth something at him that he could not make out, so he scowled, hoping she would take that as disinterest, and turned back to the discussion between Lady Alice and Summerton. He would definitely have to look out for Lady Matilda. She had entrapment on her mind, or at the very least, seduction. That part was certainly unexpected.

The relief Max felt when Diana stood up to escort the ladies to the drawing room was undeniable. However, when he looked at the other end of the table and saw his father was looking very peaked, Max stood, too. "For those of you who wish to stay behind and drink port, you are welcome to do so. I think, however, that we may relax the rules a little during this party. Consider yourselves at liberty to go where you will."

A couple of the older men looked at him with surprise, but accepted the port and settled into conversation. Max went to his father.

"Would you like to retire, sir? You look a little tired," he said quietly in his ear.

"I think I will. There has been more excitement in one day than I've had in the last three years." He chuckled lightly, but pushed himself to his feet. He further shocked Max by holding on to his arm, then bid farewell to the remaining guests. They seemed to understand and made no objections.

It was a long walk to the Duke's quarters, and Max wondered if they should find somewhere more convenient to put him for these festivities. He would see that was done in readiness for the times when the Duke did not wish to walk so far.

The Duke's valet was waiting for him when he arrived, and looked relieved to see his master. "Your Grace, you have overdone yourself!" the long-time retainer scolded, but it was evident it was only from concern.

"Nonsense, Hartley. But I am ready to retire now."

Max turned to go, but the Duke stopped him. "Thank you for this, Max. But I will never forgive you if you marry Lady Alice."

Max laughed. "You need not concern yourself on that score, Father."

"Miss Whitford, on the other hand, is enchanting."

Max smiled. He could not deny it. "Did you truly serve with her father, or was that for the benefit of the Duchess?"

"Oh, yes," the Duke replied with a twinkle in his eyes, not actually answering either question to satisfaction.

Max returned downstairs to join his guests, but paused when he heard laughter coming from the study.

He stopped to look inside. "Gus!" Max walked over and embraced his brother, who was there with Montford, Carew, and Freddy, enjoying a glass of brandy.

"I was just about to go and greet Father. How is he?"

Max adored his younger brother, who was formed almost in the same dark mould as himself, but with the attitude of nonchalance that came with being the second son instead of the heir.

"He has retired for the evening. You will have to see him in the morning. I confess it will be a shock to you. He is half the man his former self was. But having everyone here seems to have lifted his spirits. I am glad you came."

"No more glad than I am."

"Oxford does not agree with you?" Max asked.

"Certain parts do." He smirked. "But the studies, no."

Max shook his head, unsurprised. "Have you all abandoned the ladies already? Do not tell me everyone has retired whilst I was seeing his Grace to his chambers."

His friends exchanged guilty looks. "There are parlour games going on in the drawing room," Freddy said, "but we are protecting ourselves."

"I beg your pardon?"

Freddy explained what Miss Patience had overheard from the maid. Lady Matilda's forward looks immediately sprang to mind.

"So that is what you were discussing at dinner. I have a feeling I might be able to narrow down the suspects. It is only a suspicion, mind you, but we cannot barricade ourselves inside the study for the duration of the house party."

His brother handed him a glass of brandy and he took it gratefully. Had it only been one day—that was not yet over?

"Let me guess. The fusby-faced Wilton sister," Freddy said with uncharacteristic cynicism.

Max grinned knowingly. Freddy really did have a strong dislike of the two sisters. "On what other delights did the delightful Whitford ladies enlighten you?"

"Not much. We were also telling Gus about the row you and the Duchess had."

"Mother is still up to her old tricks, is she?"

"She has decided Miss Cunningham shall be the next Duchess of Davenmere, and no other shall do," Max confirmed.

"Vivienne?" Gus asked doubtfully.

"That's what I said," Freddy agreed.

"I suppose her Grace thinks it's time you beget an heir. I must say I wish you would so I may be off the hook." His brother threw him a mischievous glance.

"As it happens, there are a few eligible ladies here I am considering."

"Pray tell." Gus refilled his glass, then walked around the room and filled up the others.

"I do not suppose Gus has had the opportunity to meet the Whitford sisters, has he?" Carew asked.

"I have not. Are they here?"

Max sank into a chair and took a long drink of his brandy while his friends told Gus about their Season, culminating with Westwood's marriage to the eldest sister, Faith.

CHAPTER 7

The next morning, the men were to go fishing, and the ladies were to go shopping in the village. The afternoon would offer a variety of lawn games, followed by a picnic along the river.

Since Hope and her sisters did not wish to go shopping, they decided to take some books and read in the Roman bath house.

Jenkins came into Hope's bedchamber to help her dress, and another maid followed with a tray of chocolate and rolls. Hope wondered if this was normal for house parties or just part of life in a ducal mansion. She had not even ordered anything to break her fast, as she was engaged to eat downstairs with her sisters. The chocolate smelled divine and the rolls were still warm. Sadly, she didn't care for the taste of chocolate. She bit into a soft, buttery roll. How easily she could get used to this, she thought wryly.

She sat on a chair on the small balcony while she waited for her sisters. The cool dew had vaporized into a mist over the meadow, which smelled fresh and earthy. Rays from the rising sun shone over the peak behind her like a blessing, and she could hear the river running away towards the meadow. She sighed with contentment and began to wonder about the note she'd received the night before. Was she being tested, threatened or admired? Perhaps she should ask her sisters.

"May I drink your chocolate?" Joy asked as her sisters entered her chambers like another force of nature. Joy was already helping herself without waiting for an answer.

"Help yourself," Hope answered with an ironic twist of her lips.

"This is lovely," Grace said, walking out on to the balcony and leaning forward to look at the view.

"Frankly, I am surprised the Duchess didn't have me put in the dungeon," Hope teased.

"There is a dungeon?" Joy asked with a little too much interest.

"I do not think she had a say in this," Patience remarked as she plucked the remaining roll from the tray and broke it in half and offered Grace the other. "Why did you order breakfast in here? Are we not eating together?"

"I did not order it. Never fear, I am happy to eat more with you. As you know, I do not like chocolate and need my tea!"

"That is odd. Perhaps the maid delivered it to the wrong room."

They giggled at the thought that they had eaten someone else's food.

"Shall we go? I cannot wait to choose something from the library," Grace said. "I hear it boasts ten thousand volumes!"

"Perhaps we should eat first, then choose. I do not care to be the one that spills tea on one of the Duke's first editions." Gads, Hope was beginning to sound like Faith.

"I suppose you are right."

They wound their way through the maze of the house, passing maids hurrying to bring their mistresses hot water and towels or the chambermaids performing their duties.

It did take a small army to run a place like this. Did the Duchess oversee every detail? Or was it a competent housekeeper? Hope wondered. Certainly it was no small feat to make a party such as this run smoothly.

They filled their plates from the side-tables, which overflowed with pastries, fruits, eggs, and an assortment of meats from kippers to bacon and sausages. They chose one of the tables set out on the terrace, overlooking the gardens. In a way, Hope was relieved to be able to relax a bit and not feel like she was being watched. Perhaps the note had been a threat, after all.

There were not many guests still breakfasting. Hope assumed the men had already gone fishing and the ladies had either not come down or were already shopping. "Do you think the Duchess has to plan all the meals and activities?" she asked.

"I thought Lady Diana was the hostess."

"Let me guess, the maid told you? Jenkins is very close-lipped when she is helping me."

"Perhaps you need to encourage her more," Joy said. "I hear the nurses saying all sorts of things when I am upstairs with Susan."

"Do you care to share?" Patience prodded.

Joy gave a playful shrug of one shoulder and sneaked the cat a piece of kipper. He was hiding in a pocket that Joy had fashioned on the front of her gown. "I do not pay attention most of the time. Is there something in particular you wish to know?"

Patience sighed with exaggeration and looked heavenward. "I want to know everything!"

"Perhaps you should ask Susan. She pays much more mind than I do. But I will try to remember when we go to visit the puppies this afternoon."

"But first, let us go find something to read in the library." They entered the house and asked directions. Hope remembered where a library was, but she wanted to make certain that was the one available to guests. The butler was kind enough to escort them there and assure them they were welcome to choose anything they liked.

Rarely did anything render the four of them speechless at once, but this library did. Books and periodicals had been prized commodities at Halbury, and the look she'd had into the room from the hall had only been a hint. Once they turned the corner, it opened up into a magnificent double-height row of bookshelves lined with row upon row of leather-bound tomes, their gilded spines gleaming in the soft light seeping in through the large, mullioned windows. The scent of old parchment and leather filled the air, and inviting velvet chairs and sofas dotted the room as an invitation to stay and enjoy oneself.

"How can one person have so many books?" Grace asked. "I do not think I would ever leave this room!"

"You have at least two weeks to read as many as you can," Hope said with amusement.

"But I do not know where to start. There are so many!"

"Do you think they have the new book by Frances Burney?" Joy asked. "Miss Hillier has not been able to find it yet at Hookham's."

Hope looked around and tried to find a pattern to the book order, but all she could find were history books. "Perhaps we should ask? They might not have novels."

"Surely they must. I do not think there can be only boring old history books with so many in the collection—unless there are duplicates on the higher shelves."

Just then, Rotham strode into the library from the far side, looking intently at something in his hand. He was dressed casually in tall leather boots, riding breeches, and shirt-sleeves. His hair was ruffled as though he'd been running his hands through it, not at all like the normally immaculate London Beau Hope was used to. Immediately, she felt warm inside. How could he be more handsome when dishevelled?

He stopped when he saw them and made a quick bow. "Ladies."

They bobbed quick curtsies in greeting. Were they all as affected by him as she?

"Do you have novels, Rotham?" Joy asked, straight to the point. No one ever caused her to forget her words.

"Of course. Claudia keeps them over here."

He rounded the corner to some shelves that were more hidden from public view.

Grace exclaimed at the vision before her. "Look, Joy! They have all the latest volumes. That confirms it. I am not leaving the library for my entire stay."

"You are welcome to take them anywhere you wish, Miss Grace," Rotham said with amusement.

Hope stood back and watched as her sisters greedily helped themselves to stacks of books. Rotham came to stand next to her.

"You did not go fishing with the other gentlemen, my lord?"

He held up the paper in his hand. "I intended to, but alas, something urgent needed my attention first. You did not wish to shop with the other ladies?"

"There is plenty of shopping to be had in London. We thought to spend the morning reading in the bath house. Lady Diana suggested it."

"It is one of my favourite places to read as well. If you will allow me to give this to Abernathy, I will escort you there. It is on my way to the fishing pool."

Hope watched him leave through yet another entrance, presumably to where Abernathy waited, that individual being, she guessed, the estate manager.

Rotham returned a few minutes later with his hair neatly combed and wearing a loose, dark coat. 'Twas not quite dinner party attire, but he was less unkempt than before. She wished the rest of the guests to the devil so she could have him thus relaxed and all to herself.

Being his duchess would be like that, she reminded herself. He had duties to hundreds of other people, even in the country. Could she bear being second to his duties?

Rotham guided them through one of the wings of the house and out of a side door. They stopped by the gamekeeper's hut, as he called it, to collect his fishing gear. It was a beautiful stone building in keeping with the rest of the house.

They walked on towards the woods, which were full of mature trees, including oaks and elms, that provided shade and a sense of age and history to the landscape.

"And this is the bath house." It was part conservatory, part bath house. One entire wall was made of glass and overlooked the river. The room was filled with plants, and it was warm and damp inside to foster their growth, he explained. At the centre, the famed mosaic was encased beneath a glass floor for preservation, and was a perfectly preserved image of Herculaneum surrounded by mermaids in bright tiles of blue and green.

A great place to escape reality. Hope immediately thought it was the best place she had ever been as she inhaled the scent of oranges, and understood the previous Duke's obsession.

"There is also a bathing room, but the fires must be stoked higher to make the water warm enough. At present, they are kept smouldering enough to keep the plants growing. The plants were a later addition by the sixth Duchess."

Her sisters hurried to claim their spots as if there weren't enough to choose from, she mused, looking around at the dozen nooks and chaise longues and even a couple of swings within the indoor garden.

Rotham grabbed her hand and tugged her. "This way," he whispered.

He led her to a hidden alcove, in which another glass floor covered flowing water. She could see the water run on down the valley from there.

"This is my preferred spot," he said, with a wink and a bow. "Until later."

Hope sat on the green-cushioned seat and watched him leave. Not once did she open the book in her lap.

Rotham had no desire to fish. He wanted to climb into that alcove with Hope and wile away the afternoon there with her and...those were dangerous thoughts.

This morning had been nothing if not a pointed reminder of what becoming duke would entail. Instead of fishing with the other gentlemen, he'd had to deal with an irate tenant over a boundary dispute. His time was no longer solely his own purview.

But the moment he had seen Hope, he'd relaxed, and everything had felt right. She seemed to belong at Davenmere, regardless of what her Grace thought. Was that enough? Was he being selfish?

He walked on down to where the gentlemen were fishing, a slow point in the river that formed a small pool, where a dozen of the gentlemen were casting lures. Some were in the water and some on the bank.

"They are not biting this morning, Max," his father said from a chair on the shore.

"Perhaps you will bring good luck," Summerton called over the dull sound of the moving water.

Max saw a tug on the line and the old man roared with pleasure. "Will you look at that!" His father held up a small brown trout that was thrashing back and forth.

Max congratulated him and walked over to his friends.

"What held you up?" Montford asked.

"A tenant dispute," he answered blandly.

"Let me guess. Old man Byford and Farmer Jeffers?" Freddy asked.

"Indeed." Max furrowed his brow. "How did you know?"

"Because they have taken their grievances to my father as well. The other side of their properties border ours. Father sent them straight back to Abernathy."

Frankly, Max was surprised that Freddy knew more about the tenants than he did.

"How did you handle them?" Carew asked as he reeled in a carp, then unhooked it before tossing it into the waiting basket.

"I told him it would probably be best if one of them moved away from the other. That way they would not have any more disputes."

"And did they agree?"

"Actually, Jeffers did. He agreed to move to a farm on the other side of the estate once this growing season ends."

"And here I thought you'd been a-wooing this morning," Carew mused.

"Wooing would have been far more pleasant…although I did just see the Whitford ladies to the bath house. They found some volumes of interest in the library they wanted to read."

"Are you not going to fish?" Freddy asked, inclining his head towards the pole in Max's hand.

"Maybe another day. I think I'd rather walk. I will join you this afternoon." His friends didn't protest and waved him on. After handing his equipment to his father's footman, he thrust his hands in his pockets and walked on along the river bank. It had been years since he had spent any length of time at Davenmere. Normally it felt like a trap, but now? Perhaps he had matured and was accepting his fate.

He wandered far away from the gathering and became lost in his thoughts. He found himself back near the bath house and shook his head. If it was simply an infatuation, it would pass. But how would he know if it was more than that? He liked Hope—and he could not recall ever liking another female as a friend at the same time as wanting her.

"My lord!" a female voice called out to him as if startled, and he looked around.

"Lady Matilda." How had he allowed himself to be caught unawares?

She tittered. "I thought you were fishing with the other gentlemen."

"I have just come from there," he replied, though he suspected she knew very well what he'd been doing. "Why are you out here alone?"

"I have lost my way. Could you help me find my way back?" She blinked her eyes up at him as though she was about to produce tears. He'd been tricked too many times to fall for the ploy. He hesitated, not wanting to arrive back at the house alone with her. He knew very well there would be someone lying in wait to catch them together.

Max looked at the bath house, warring with asking for help. Of course he should. Had they not explained the dilemma to the sisters? Of course, it was still humiliating to be caught in such a position. "Of course, I will help, but let me inform the other ladies. I told them I would make sure everything was to their satisfaction," he prevaricated. He did not miss the flash of annoyance in her eyes before he turned towards the building which housed his salvation. As he climbed the steps, he saw Miss Hope watching him from the alcove. His plea for help must have been written all over his face, because she nodded and rose to come towards him.

He opened the door to find Patience, Grace, and Joy so engrossed in their books that they did not even look up at him.

"There you are, my lord," Hope said with a bright smile, bless her.

"We have a slight change in plans. Lady Matilda has lost her way and needs a guide back to the house. Do you mind?"

They exchanged knowing glances.

"Of course not, sir. Let me tell my sisters."

Patience and Grace barely acknowledged her, but Joy moaned. Something about her did not look right.

"Joy?" Hope asked.

The youngest Whitford grunted in response. Max moved closer.

"She looks ill."

Hope knelt down and put her hand on Joy's face. "She does not feel feverish."

Max thought she looked a little green himself, but he was no doctor.

"Pain." Joy pointed to her stomach.

"Perhaps you had too much chocolate. We will return to the house."

She nodded miserably, but when she tried to stand, she doubled over, grasping her middle.

Max bent over and scooped her into his arms. Thankfully, she was light and she held on to his neck. When they came down the stairs where Lady Matilda was waiting, it was clear she had not expected company on their return.

"Miss Joy has fallen ill. Forgive my haste."

He hurried as fast as he could without jarring Joy. He didn't look back to see if Lady Matilda was keeping up. She had found her way there, she could find her way back.

As they entered the house, he instructed Gilford to send for the doctor.

He carried Joy up to her chambers and placed her on the bed.

"Leave me," she choked out.

Max took that as a sign that she needed privacy. Hope was right behind him as they left the room.

"She has been through so much. Hopefully, this is something minor," Hope said in a worried tone.

"Do you think her food was spoiled?" he asked, worrying over a problem in his kitchens.

"The only thing she had which we did not was the chocolate that had been sent to my room this morning."

"And you did not have any?"

She shook her head. "Neither did my sisters. I do not care for it."

Max frowned. It was probably some sour milk or something one of the cows had eaten had tainted the milk. It had happened before when one of the dairy cows had become loose and gorged itself in the meadow on wild onions.

One of the chambermaids passed by, and he asked her to send up Mrs. Watson.

"Yes, my lord." She bobbed a curtsy and hurried away.

Some retching sounds began coming from Joy's room and Hope looked at him with anguish. "I should go to her."

Max nodded. "I'll send the doctor in as soon as he arrives."

Mrs. Watson hurried up to them a minute or two later and Max told her what had happened.

"To my knowledge, my lord, the only guests who requested breakfast in their chambers were Lady Wilton and her daughters. I will have some fresh water and linens sent up until Dr. Cafferty arrives and tells us what else to do. I pray it's not a contagion."

Max nodded in absolute agreement as she returned down the hall. Was it wrong to hope it would be a reason to send the other guests away? He waited outside the door for another half an hour before the doctor arrived. If Miss Joy had anything left inside her tiny person, he would be very much surprised.

When the physician came back out to speak with Max, he was shaking his head.

"How is she?"

"If it is only sour milk, it will pass quickly. If it is something worse, like cholera or dysentery, it will be much longer. I have left a draught to help relieve the spasms, but she must continue to drink. It is the lack of fluids that deteriorates people in these situations, you know."

Max did not know. "Is there a risk to the rest of the household?"

"Maybe so, maybe not. It is too soon for me to say. Best to be careful and keep her in her rooms."

Immediately, Max thought of his father. Something like this would kill him quickly.

He nodded and saw the doctor out, praying it was nothing more than sour milk.

CHAPTER 8

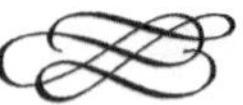

*J*oy was in agonizing pain for a few hours, but the retching seemed to have stopped, and she was resting now, thank God. Miss Hillier was sitting with her so that Hope could rest and possibly join the others for the afternoon. Hope was not sure if she could be jovial after what her sister had just gone through. Poor Joy.

Hope returned to her room and went to splash her face with water, then take down her hair. A folded piece of paper on the dressing table caught her eye. Nervously, she opened it.

Your beauty daunts and ensnares affections, but are secrets concealed?

Hope dropped the paper back on the dressing table, her hands trembling. Again, the note could be admiration, but it felt like a threat. It certainly did not feel like a compliment.

She shook her head and took a deep breath. Was she overreacting? She picked it up again to examine it. The paper was of good quality, but nondescript. There was no fragrance, and the script was bold and elegant—nothing that would identify its author as either male or female. She folded the note back the way it had been and placed it in her pocket.

Instead of resting, she redressed her hair in a simple knot, added the first note to her pocket as well and then went to find her sisters. She had to tell someone.

Hope tried to remember where the games were taking place, and she thought she had heard they would be on the south lawn. She wound her way through the wings, only having to stop to ask a servant for directions once, and passed through the doors to lush, rolling lawns stretched out before the house, surrounded by a profusion of carefully landscaped gardens. The gardens featured an array of vibrant flowers, neatly trimmed hedges, and winding pathways for leisurely strolls. Ornate fountains, charming gazebos, and serene ponds adorned with water lilies completed the scene.

There were tennis courts where a couple of the gentlemen were hitting a small ball back and forth over a net with wooden spoon-shaped rackets, to the amusement of several ladies watching.

Grace was trying her hand at archery under the direction of Lord Carew, along with Lady Agatha and Lord Rotham. Hope was determined not to be jealous or envious as she heard Lady Agatha simper at an excellent shot his lordship had made.

Continuing on, she found Patience playing lawn bowls with Lord Augustus, Lord Brosner and Lady Alice against Mr. Cunningham and his sister, as well as Lord Montford and his sister, Lady Caroline. It was looking like a heated competition. She would have been highly amused by it were she not so exhausted and worried about the letter.

"Would you care to join us, Miss Whitford?" Lord Brosner asked with a friendly smile.

"Oh, no, indeed, sir, thank you. That would spoil the pairings. I am happy to watch."

"If you change your mind, you can share turns with me." He picked up his wooden ball and rolled it down the green, landing very near the jack.

"Well done, my lord." Politely, she acknowledged the expertly placed ball.

"How is Joy?" Patience asked when she finished her turn and spotted Hope.

"She is resting now. Hopefully, the worst has passed. The doctor said if it was simply the chocolate, then she will improve quickly. Miss Hillier is sitting with her now and will alert me if she becomes ill again."

"What is wrong with Miss Joy?" Mr. Cunningham asked. He must have overheard.

Hope exchanged glances with Patience. "She has been taken ill. We believe she drank something that did not agree with her."

"That is a lot of rotten luck for one young lady," he said with concern.

Hope agreed. Joy had not long recovered from her accident with a horse earlier in the spring. "Pray it is over with now. She is resting," she assured Mr. Cunningham.

"Are you almost finished?" Hope asked her sister, trying not to appear as agitated as she felt.

Patience looked at her oddly. "I can be if Lord Montford does not knock my bowl out of the way."

"I always follow the rules, Miss Patience," Montford objected.

Mr. Cunningham snorted. "And that's the truth!"

Montford stepped up to the line and rolled his bowl, just missing the jack.

Hope watched as her very competitive sister stepped up to take her turn, then knocked Montford's off the green, leaving hers in its place.

Patience grinned with triumph. "Now, what did you need me for?"

Hope shook her head at her sister's antics. "Let us find Grace first, so I do not need to repeat myself."

Again, Hope had to wait for Grace to finish her archery lesson. She looked none too pleased to be pulled away from Carew's attentions, but she did follow along.

"What is it?" Grace asked. "Is Joy worse?"

Hope explained what had happened and what the doctor had said.

"You should have sent for us!" Patience scolded.

"What could you have done but watch her misery? I am telling you now, but that is not what I wanted to discuss with you." She led them away from the others to one of the marble follies. There was a statue, a replica of the goddess Venus, inside.

"They really are interested in Roman history here," Patience observed dryly. "I suppose if I never get to visit Italy, I will not feel completely deprived."

Too upset to be amused, Hope took the notes from her pocket and opened them.

"What is that?" Grace asked.

"Notes left in my room." She handed one to each of her sisters.

They read them, then looked at her in confusion as they handed them back.

"There was nothing else?"

"No. Plain paper, no scent, indeterminate handwriting…"

"They seem admiring, yet not," Patience observed.

"How odd," Grace agreed.

"How disturbing," Hope corrected. "I wondered if it was just my imagination, but my instinct tells me otherwise."

"What are you going to do?" Grace asked.

"What can I do? I can hardly announce to the entire household that someone is sending me secret letters. The Duchess already thinks I am an encroaching hussy." Hope paced in a circle around the folly.

"How is it your fault if someone is sending you notes? Do you think they could be from Rotham and he simply needs lessons in articulation?" Patience propped herself up next to the statue.

"I only wish that were the case, but I would look a fool if I walked up to him and asked. I cannot do it." Hope shook her head.

"I wish Faith was here. She would know what to do," Grace bemoaned, and Hope agreed.

"I do not see why we cannot ask the gentlemen for help. They would know what to do. I do not think any of them would have written notes in such a clandestine fashion. Although, perhaps Carew…" Patience considered, deep in thought.

"Not Carew!" Grace protested.

"I agree. Carew has no real interest in me. He is only trying to help make Rotham jealous."

"It worked with Westwood," Patience conceded.

"So you think I should just ignore these?" She held up the offensive objects.

"They are not threatening."

"I suppose not. They have certainly unsettled me, nevertheless."

"Then do not go anywhere alone. The gentlemen made a pact to protect each other, and I think we should as well."

"Observe that Rotham was almost caught by Lady Matilda this morning," Hope pointed out.

"Precisely."

"I still cannot think who would do such a thing!" Hope threw her hands up.

"Maybe one of the other ladies is jealous and sent them out of spite," Patience suggested.

"Along with sour chocolate that was meant for me?" Hope asked doubtfully. "No. Who would be jealous of me?"

"Someone who doesn't know you dislike chocolate. Lady Matilda, for instance."

"That was just an unfortunate coincidence." Hope dismissed the thought. She could not even begin to think anyone would put a person through something like that deliberately, although Lady Matilda could possibly have an incentive. Desperation could cause drastic behaviours.

"I think we should tell the Dowager and the maids, at the very least. They see things and are around when we are not," Patience suggested.

"They were certainly bold enough to go into my room. The second note was on my dressing table," Hope explained.

"And the first?" Grace asked.

"It was slipped under my door when I was in the room. I hurried to look, but they were already gone."

"So the second note was put there while we were at the bath house. That was several hours ago. Yet the ladies were shopping and the gentlemen were fishing. It should be simple enough to see who stayed behind." Patience was thinking aloud.

"We know that Rotham did," Grace pointed out.

Hope shook her head. "I still cannot think he would write that way —it does not seem in his style."

"Jenkins can find out, although it could have been someone's servant."

"True," Hope said. "I just need to know. I will run mad with suspecting everyone otherwise."

Patience took her hand and squeezed sympathetically, while Grace hugged her.

"I do feel better, having told you," Hope confessed.

"Why would you not have told us?" Patience retorted.

"I thought I might be overreacting."

"It always feels better to share things," Grace said innocently.

"Hopefully, there will be no more notes," Hope said, though she did not believe this was the end of it. "I should go and visit Joy."

"Miss Hillier can be trusted. She will send for us if Joy needs something." Patience stopped her.

"I know you are right, but I feel as though Faith would have stayed by her side."

"No one expects you to be just like Faith," Patience scoffed.

If only Hope did not feel that somehow she was failing.

Lady Agatha *was* fusby-faced, though Max would never admit to his friends that they had been correct. Selecting the proper duchess did not always proffer the luxury of that lady also being a beauty. When the party had met on the south lawn for games, everyone had begun to divide into the various activities.

Summerton and Wilton opposed each other across the net, and most of the matrons watched from chairs placed beneath the shade of a nearby oak. The young adults chose shuttlecock, whilst Max's friends elected lawn bowls. He thought that a fine idea, but when he stepped forward to join the others, Lady Wilton moved in front of him.

"My lord, Lady Agatha has always wanted to learn archery, have you not, my dear?"

"Yes, of course, Mama." That lady smiled shyly with a nervous simper.

"I have heard you are an expert, and who better to instruct a novice than you?" Lady Wilton tittered.

It was the perfect opportunity, and he had not had to try to orchestrate time with her, which was even better. "I would be delighted, Lady Agatha."

"Off with you, then," Lady Wilton said as though eager for them to be on their way.

"I would also like to learn." Miss Grace boldly stepped forward, bless her. She was taking the protection bit to heart.

"I am certain someone else would be happy to teach you as well," Lady Agatha said, obviously none too pleased at having to share.

"I am mediocre at best, but I would be more than happy to show you what I know," Carew graciously offered.

"Wonderful!" Lady Agatha said a bit too exuberantly.

His eyes met Carew's, and he saw understanding. He wanted to have a chance to speak with Lady Agatha, not be cornered and forced into anything.

They walked on down to the archery range, where the targets had been set up, and footmen brought quivers of arrows for each of them.

Lady Agatha went over to select a bow. Of course, she selected the largest, strongest one.

"Perhaps you might wish to begin with something a little smaller, Lady Agatha," Max suggested.

She giggled. "How silly of me!"

Max smiled. "Permit me to help you." Quickly, he ascertained the shyness had been feigned. She was nothing of the sort. Every chance she could, she bumped into him. She was constantly grabbing his arm and trying to step right next to him. It was no surprise, when it came time to position the arrow and shoot it, that she could not manage without Max's help.

"Perhaps she is very near-sighted?" Carew drawled in a brief reprieve while they went down the range to examine their own shots.

"You are very generous. I feel smothered."

Max noticed that Miss Grace was a natural and was already hitting the target with her arrows.

"Just imagine a lifetime of scintillating conversation," Carew warned.

"Any conversation would be welcome," Max retorted as he yanked the arrows from the target.

When he returned to his partner, he was determined to make an effort to draw her out. Perhaps this was just her mother's influence, and she would be better alone. How long was it until the picnic?

Every topic of conversation or question he posed resulted in the answer, "What do you think, my lord?" He resigned himself to an afternoon of batting eyelashes, mundane conversation, simpering and forced proximity. He didn't know why he was surprised by any of it. 'Twas all part of the game, after all, but it was quickly obvious Lady Agatha was not the one for him.

If he had not been wishing that the lady in his arms was someone else, it might have been less tedious. He'd never seen Hope behave as vulgarly as Lady Agatha was doing. Why did the Duchess think that pedigree mattered more than behaviour? However, he had wanted the opportunity to fairly evaluate all of the other ladies, and other than Lady Caroline, he'd done so. She would be his next object. It was difficult not to hold all others up against Hope, even though most thought it should be the other way around.

His only consolation was Carew was in a similar situation with Miss Grace. At least she was not fusby-faced.

Thus far, he had managed to escape his mother. He was trying very hard to keep her from knowledge of his thoughts or intentions. The less dealings they had with each other, the better. But she was present on the lawns that afternoon and was certainly not stupid.

He hoped all that she could see was him being a cordial host. He had actually spent very little time with Hope—certainly no one could say he had singled her out.

The Duke seemed to be having a grand time, and planned to take the hounds out the next morning. Even if Max did not narrow down a bride in time, he had made his father happy, as opposed to the Duchess, who was never happy. Such commonplace emotions were beneath her.

As the games were ending and the picnic was being laid out, Max spied Hope walking back towards the house with her sisters and he wondered how Joy was doing.

He turned to follow them to find out. A hand on his arm stopped him.

"Rotham."

He only just stopped himself from emitting a heavy sigh. "Your Grace."

He turned around and looked down at his mother, whose eyes were following the Whitford ladies' movements.

"Are you leaving your guests before the picnic?"

"I intend to return as soon as possible, but there is something that needs attending to. Diana and the servants have everything well in hand."

"Indeed." Her voice indicated she thought she knew exactly what he was going to attend to.

He did not wish to explain himself. Grovelling like a sniffling schoolboy would give her too much power. "The sooner I go, the sooner I may return."

"What is so urgent that you must go at once?" she asked scornfully.

Would she have questioned his father in such a manner? Of course not.

"If you must know, one of the guests has taken ill. If you will excuse me?"

"You are making a fool of yourself, Rotham." Her voice dripped with bitterness.

"Then that makes two of us, I suppose." He turned on his heel and returned to the house, determined not to let his mother infuriate him.

His primary concern was for Miss Joy's welfare, and if that made him look a fool, then so be it.

He entered via the front door in order to speak to Gilford to discover if there had been any change. "Has it been necessary to send for the doctor again, Gilford?"

"Not to my knowledge, my lord."

He then found Mrs. Watson as he traversed the house. "Has there been any change in Miss Joy?" he asked.

"The last I heard, things had settled, and she was resting, my lord," she answered in her stiff manner.

"That is excellent news, thank you."

"I did question the servants, sir. No one else has fallen ill," she added.

"Thank goodness."

Max went on through to the east wing, wondering what could have happened to Joy. He knocked lightly on the sitting room to the Whitford sisters' apartments, hoping he was not disturbing her rest.

Hope opened the door.

"How is she?" he asked softly.

"She is still resting. Almost two hours have passed since she has been ill." Hope looked relieved, but also as if she had the weight of the world on her shoulders.

Max wanted to take her in his arms, but he settled for taking her hands in his, and giving them a reassuring squeeze. "You should rest."

She smiled half-heartedly.

"Is something else troubling you?"

Her eyes darted away. She was hesitating. "No, I am only concerned for Joy. Pray the worst is over."

"Will you be returning to the picnic?"

"Are you in need of an escort, Rotham?" she teased.

"I am afraid for my virtue," he quipped.

"There are some rather determined ladies here."

They laughed, then caught each other's gaze. It felt so right and easy to be with her. "And you, Hope? Are you determined?" They leaned towards each other. He was tired of fighting his attraction to her. What would it feel like to kiss her?

"Rotham!" Grace said as she burst into the room.

Guiltily, Max and Hope jumped apart. He had almost kissed her in the room next to that of her sisters, where Joy lay ill. What kind of a scoundrel was he?

"Is there any change?" he asked Grace, and could feel Hope's eyes upon him. Did she know she had almost been kissed? They had never crossed the bounds of friendship, but there had always been an easy flirtation there. It did not help that the papers always put them together in their speculations and caricatures.

"She is still resting, though she did wake for a short time and took some of the draught the doctor prescribed. Patience and I are going to return to the picnic. Miss Hillier insists she is content to stay with Joy and read."

"Very well. Then I have three escorts to protect me," he said with a smile as the little orange tabby cat came up and rubbed himself on Max's ankles. He picked him up and was rewarded with a purr.

"Maybe he needs to go outside," Hope said and taking the cat from him, found one of the pouches Joy sometimes carried him in.

"I am surprised to find you alone after this morning, Rotham," Patience said as she entered the room. "Lady Matilda had her hooks into you."

"I followed you three inside. You were within earshot the whole time." Max laughed, but it was not amusing in the least.

He and Hope followed Patience and Grace in a natural pairing as they walked back through the house and gardens and out to where the picnic had been set up near the lake. Even though he longed to stay with the Whitford sisters, he could feel his mother's eyes upon him and so left their side when they reached the other guests.

CHAPTER 9

hen they reached the picnic, Rotham excused himself
and went to speak with another group of guests. Hope
tried not to feel disappointed or watch him as he walked away like a
starving dog waiting for crumbs. Of course, he could not always stay
by her side when he was hosting so many people.

Her gaze caught the Dowager's and she smiled but then Hope saw
the Duchess sitting next to the Viscountess, glaring. At least, it seemed
to be a glare. Hope had never seen her Grace look pleasant, so perhaps
that was her normal expression.

How she could have brought up such an affable son as a Rotham
was beyond her, though Hope knew most of the nobility's children
were raised by nurses and governesses, then school and tutors.

Hope filled her plate, but did not feel hungry. She felt as though
she were an intruder as she and her sisters sat at a table with Vivienne
Cunningham and Lady Susan Courtenay.

"Patience! Grace! You will never believe what I have heard!" Miss
Cunningham said with such innocent exuberance that Hope
wondered if she'd ever been that childlike. "The Dowager has received
word that our friends from the Regiment in London have been given
some leave and they are to visit for a few days!"

"And Rotham has said we may have a ball while they are here!" Lady Susan added.

Immediately, they began to chatter about their friends in the Guards and how grand it would be to have more dancing partners.

Why could Hope not feel as excited as they did?

As they discussed the ball, Hope casually looked around, wondering who had sent her the notes. The Duchess and the Dowager were talking and, thankfully, she had looked away. However, as she scanned the tables of guests, Lady Matilda was watching her with menace.

What was Hope doing wrong? Why were so many ladies here against her? Possibly her sisters were right that it was simple jealousy. What did she have that they did not, except perhaps, beauty? But beauty was in the eye of the beholder, and apparently not enough to make a person suited to be a duchess.

Hope had never understood jealousy. Wanting what someone else had, perhaps, could be understood, but to wish others ill for your gain? If they only knew that there was nothing at all for them to be jealous of, she thought sadly.

She started as she realized the Dowager was approaching her.

"Have you finished eating? I wondered if you would care for a stroll about the lake?"

"Of course," Hope said, standing up. Her ladyship took Hope's arm as if to say we are going for a simple stroll, but Hope knew there was something she wanted to discuss. Had the Duchess told her to warn Hope away?

They walked down the hill, but the Dowager did not say anything until they reached the edge of the water. A warm breeze blew their skirts and lifted their bonnets a little as they stood on a berm near the shore.

"Is something the matter?"

"I was sitting with the Duchess," the Dowager began as the water lapped at the bank.

"She does not care for us, I think."

The Dowager laughed lightly. "That is her way. I do not think I have ever known her to like anyone particularly."

That was a small comfort. Hope felt even more sadness for Lord Rotham. She had not known her parents long, but at least she'd known laughter and love from them.

"The Duchess did make mention of some interesting things."

Hope looked up expectantly.

"She says the Duke will cut Rotham off if he does not marry as they wish."

"Cut him off? Do you mean disinherit him?" Hope asked, shocked to her core.

"Indeed. He promised his father he would choose a bride soon since the Duke's health is failing."

"But he says he will not be forced to marry Miss Cunningham," Hope insisted.

The Dowager Viscountess turned towards Hope and looked at her with sympathy. "Has he singled you out?"

Hope thought of their too-few interactions. She shook her head. He had shown her nothing more than friendship. Although she had thought he was going to kiss her earlier, he hadn't.

"He has paid marked attention to several ladies thus far," the Dowager said gently.

Hope's face burned with recognition as she thought about it. She looked back up the hill at the gathering and saw him speaking with Lady Caroline. The Dowager was right. "Did the Duchess ask you to speak with me?"

"No, but I suspect that was her aim. Be that as it may, I know you, and I know how close you have become to Rotham. I do not wish for you to be hurt."

"I think it is too late for that," Hope confessed.

"I am sorry for it, my dear."

The look of pity she gave her only deepened the hurt she felt, and Hope only wanted to be alone in her misery. The house party had barely begun. How long was she to endure it?

"I know it will be difficult, but keep a smile on your face," the Dowager said. "Once we leave, it will be easier."

Hope nodded with a false smile. Any words would be trite. She debated whether or not she should confide in the Dowager about the notes she had been receiving. Her sisters had not been overly concerned, so perhaps she should wait.

"Shall we return?" the Dowager asked, drawing Hope's attention back to her.

"I think I will stay here a little longer, if you do not mind."

"Of course," the Dowager said with a look of understanding. That was the last thing Hope wanted. She turned and walked along the shore until she reached a rocky outcrop and sat on it. She knew she was being unsociable at the moment, but she could not face the other guests with the Duchess there, looking upon her with both scorn and satisfaction. She had to have known that the Dowager would repeat her words to Hope.

It was difficult not to chafe at the unfairness of it all. She was still a lady, even if she was not born into the nobility. Her behaviour was above reproach, and she had not thrown herself at Rotham's feet as she had seen some of the others do.

It mattered not. There was little she could do to change the Duke or Duchess's minds, even though she strongly suspected it was all the latter's doing. The Duke was a kind old man who had not seemed in the least pretentious about her father.

All she could do was her best and remain above reproach. If noble birth was the main qualification for Max's bride, then there was nothing to be done, but her pride demanded she at least behave as well or better than the others.

A large boulder that was perfect for contemplation seemed to appear in front of her, so she perched upon it. A little squawk reminded her that Freddy Tiger was with her, and she reached down to let him out. He wandered off into the grass, and Hope stretched out her feet and loosened her bonnet strings. There would be no wallowing, she told herself. She was a Whitford and her name was as fine as any other.

Freddy Tiger was leaping and pouncing after a grasshopper, and Hope had to smile at his antics. If only she had stayed by Joy's side, her happiness might have lasted a little bit longer. "No. It would have only delayed the inevitable." She sighed.

"No! Freddy, no!" Hope called, suddenly realizing the kitten was perilously close to the water's edge. Did kittens know how to swim? She had no idea, and she did not wish to find out. She climbed down from the rock to go after him.

However, the little orange ball of fluff was not listening, being determined on his object. Even the water did not deter him. He leaped and pounced and splashed right into the muddy bank, shooting clumps of mud all over Hope.

"Oh, no, you don't!" She lunged and grabbed for the cat, which only made him think she was playing a game. She chased and grabbed, and the orange cat was covered in mud when she finally caught him.

She knew she'd made a complete and utter fool of herself, and besides the bottom of her dress being soaked, the muddy cat was now pressed against her bodice. Her bonnet was hanging down her back and her hair had escaped its pins. She was afraid to turn and look, but she could hear people coming towards her.

Quickly, she turned back to the water. She could not take Freddy to the house covered in mud, so she plunged him beneath the surface, thinking to wipe him clean.

One would have thought she was trying to torture him by the way he reacted. He made a growling noise she did not know cats could make, then climbed up her arm, shoulder and neck at an alarming rate with his claws fully extended to inflict the greatest amount of damage. He must have decided her bonnet was the safest place because she could feel the hat sagging with the weight of him.

With a heavy sigh, she turned to see her sisters, along with several of the other young members of the party, laughing hysterically.

"No good deed goes unpunished," Patience said casually. "Here, let me have the bonnet." Her sister finished untying the ribbons and took it along with the wet cat inside.

"Good show, Miss Hope," Freddy called as Rotham lent her a hand onto the shore and covered her up with his coat.

"Indeed," a cold voice said as Hope looked up to see the condescending, now familiar glare of the Duchess, who was standing close by with a dismayed Dowager.

"Thank you," she said to Rotham, then lifted her chin and walked up back the hill as though she had not just sealed her fate with utter humiliation.

MAX WATCHED Hope go back to the house with her sisters, but he did not follow. He did not want to draw more attention to the situation than it had already garnered. It would only give his mother more ammunition with regards to Hope's imagined unsuitability.

Had that happened at any other time, without the older generation being there to witness Hope's mishap, it would have been humorous. Max had watched the scene unfold and had known how it would end, but was powerless to stop it. Mischief seemed to follow the Whitford ladies wherever they went.

He felt a hand go through his arm and looked down to see his sister regarding him with pity.

"Come," she said and led him back to the house. He was now without his coat anyway, and should probably rectify that.

They went into his study, and Diana poured him a drink and pressed it into his hands. "Mother will find fault with anyone," she said, sitting in one of the chairs.

"Except her choice, you mean?" Max asked rhetorically and went to stand by the window, looking out but not seeing anything.

"I suspect she will even find fault with her. It has ever been thus."

"Does she treat Gus and Claudia this way?"

"Gus is fortunate enough to be away at school. I was extremely jealous when you left, you know. I had nothing to shield me from her."

Max had not considered what it must be like for his sisters. He had loved every moment of school, away from home.

"You seem happy with Courtenay." Max turned and studied his sister.

"I was fortunate in that my choice met with her approval. However, you are to be Duke."

"Therefore, my happiness matters not," he said dryly.

"How is your hunt going, so to speak?"

"To this point, it has been a series of eliminations." He shook his head, then took a drink.

"Pray tell," Diana said eagerly.

"There is not much to tell. Lady Matilda was following me this morning in the hopes of compromising me, I have no doubt."

"And I saw her sister's performance with archery this afternoon," she added in a sardonic tone.

"I do not even know why I thought Lady Alice might be a fit." He furrowed his brow, trying to recall why she had seemed a good idea.

"I wondered if she was on your list. She is widely known to be called a devoted Wollstonecraft follower."

"I am not asking for a passive woman with no ideas of her own, but Lady Alice seems to be quite extreme in her opinions."

"What about Lady Caroline?"

"The last option other than Miss Cunningham or Miss Whitford. She has been rather shy when I have approached her. However, she did agree to ride to hounds with me in the morning."

"What is it you hope to prove? Or are you trying to assure yourself that Miss Whitford is the one?" his sister asked very acutely.

"Mother does not think she is suited to be a duchess."

"Since when did you care what Mother thinks? But you always have wanted to please everyone. It is impossible, you know."

"I do know it, but I cannot seem to help myself. Yet whilst I chafe at the very idea of succumbing to her Grace's edicts, part of me wonders if she is not correct about Hope. Would she even be comfortable in the role?"

"What if she is not, yet she makes you happy? Perhaps she doesn't host your political dinners? Does it matter? I think not. You may reshape the role as it fits the two of you."

Max stared out of the window, considering.

"You must marry for yourself, dear brother. Being Duke is a very lonely place without the right person by your side."

"I have an excellent set of friends," he pointed out.

"Be that as it may, they are beginning to marry themselves, Westwood very happily, if what his mother says is true."

Max smiled. "Indeed."

"That being said, my maid says Miss Whitford has an admirer. She saw a servant slipping a note under her door."

Max frowned. "What is the significance of that?" he asked.

"You cannot think to be the only one to appreciate her beauty."

"Of course not. She had several offers during the Season, but did not accept any of them. Moreover, I appreciate her for more than her beauty."

"She does seem to have a lovely disposition as well," Diana agreed.

"Yes. If only displays like this afternoon did not seem to occur so often with respect to her and her sisters. Though I will admit that is the first time I have seen Miss Hope create such a spectacle."

"Come now, Max. It was not so bad. She was trying to save the cat."

"Do you see any of the other ladies finding themselves in such situations?"

"Perhaps not accidental ones, but certainly ones of their own making, which is much worse in my opinion!"

Diana was right. It was what he had been thinking himself earlier, but why did he still hesitate? Was it really some deep-seated need within him that sought his mother's approval?

Diana stood up. "Go riding with Lady Caroline in the morning, just to reassure yourself, but do not let her Grace be the reason you do not choose Miss Whitford. You are the one who must live with your choice for the rest of your life." With that sisterly wisdom, Diana left him alone to his thoughts. She was correct, of course. He still wanted to give Lady Caroline a fair chance on the morrow. At least then he would be certain he had tried his best.

However, he could not shake something Diana had said.

Who would be sending clandestine notes to Hope? Should he ask her about them? What if she was being importuned?

Max had taken it for granted that Hope would be his if he asked. The thought that she might be considering others was his own fault. However, he could hardly expect her to wait while he decided if she was good enough. He scoffed at his own thoughts, which were pompous even to his own ears.

But who could it be? Surely she was not considering Brosner? Max had not considered him to be a contender for Hope's affections.

If that was the case, he had no one to blame but himself.

CHAPTER 10

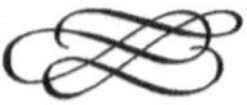

$\mathcal{A}$nother note was sitting by her wash-stand, very likely placed there by the chambermaid when she brought in her water for the morning. Hope was coming to expect them every single day now, but this one was a little different from the others.

How strong is your allure! I see how others watch you as I watch. Yet tread carefully, for not all admirers bear kind intentions.

"You don't say," Hope muttered as she read the note.

It was still a threat, but almost laced with advice. Hope shook her head. It was unnerving to have someone meddling without knowing who it was. It could not be someone close to her, for they would say what they wanted her to face. Therefore, it had to be someone outside their circle, but who? If she only knew were the writer male or female, it would help. Women tended to be more spiteful, so that was her first inclination.

There was little time to think, though, because Jenkins arrived to dress her. It was a big day, with the hunt happening, and the Duke's excitement was infectious. Hope had never liked the thought of running a fox to death, even if they didn't kill it, but as avid riders, all of the sisters enjoyed the thrill of a good gallop across the countryside with jumping fences as part of the chase.

Hope was also excited, despite the new note of warning. Perhaps she should consider other suitors? Lord Brosner had been paying her attention and he was handsome. However, he was a marquess in his own right. If she wasn't suited to be a duchess, then there was little difference in the rank of marchioness!

Jenkins held up a dark blue riding habit tailored with a high-waisted jacket and adorned with brass buttons. Then she dressed her hair in a plaited knot with a military style hat adorned with white feathers and ribbons to tie it beneath her chin.

Once she was ready, she went down the hall to find her sisters. She was surprised to find Joy up and dressed, ready to go with them.

"Joy, are you well enough?" Hope asked.

"I am not about to miss a ride, Hope. I was specifically invited by Lady Susan."

"I am only concerned if you feel up to it. Yesterday must have sapped your strength."

"It did," she conceded, still looking rather pale. "However, I was able to keep some gruel down last night and drink quite a bit of broth."

"That is excellent news. I want you to promise me that you will stop if you begin to feel weak."

"There is no need to warn me. I've had a bad fall recently, and have no wish to repeat such an event."

Hope was glad to hear it. She loved Joy's spirit, but she had ever been a neck or nothing rider.

"Shall we go?" Patience asked, standing by the door looking fetching in her own new dark green habit in the military style with frogged button-holes and braided trimmings.

They made their way to the dining room where tables of food had been set aside to sustain them through the morning. There was a hum of excitement in the air as everyone was itching to get started.

Hope was surprised to see the Duke dressed in scarlet livery. The tail-coat had obviously originally been made for a larger person, though it had been altered. From what she had heard, he was half his normal size. It must be hard for Rotham to see his father like that.

Hope was also relieved to see that the matrons had not yet come down that morning. Many ladies did not ride to hounds because of the constraints of the side-saddle. Were the Duke not such an avid hunter, and having allowed his own daughters to ride, then it was likely the Whitford sisters would not have had this opportunity. They had never ridden to hounds precisely, but were bruising riders. It was one of the few pleasures Lady Halbury had allowed them.

The large group made their way to the stables. It was early enough that the morning air was cool and a fine mist still hung over the valley, with dew still lying on the grass. There were ten gentlemen and eight ladies planning to ride that morning.

"Do you have a riding partner?" a deep voice asked as he brought his mount alongside hers.

"Lord Brosner. Good morning. In fact, I have not yet paired off with anyone."

"May I be the lucky fellow to pair with you then? Rotham has asked the gentlemen to pair with a lady, and as my sister is vehemently opposed to the sport, she will not be joining us."

"That is a shame," Hope remarked. But she knew there were many who sympathized with the fox. Gentlemen, she was learning, were highly driven by sport in any form.

Her gaze fell upon Rotham, joining forces with Lady Caroline, and she turned back to smile at Brosner. "I would be delighted to accompany you, my lord."

"Excellent." He smiled down at her, and she decided to open her mind to the possibility. If all she felt for Rotham was infatuation, it would pass, and she could possibly open her heart to someone else one day.

"Have you hunted before, Miss Whitford?" he asked.

"I have not, but I have spent a lot of time in the saddle. As I understand it, we follow the hounds, and they chase the fox?"

"Normally, yes, but it is too early to hunt foxes—there are rules about such things, you know—so we will follow hounds only," he explained.

"If there is no fox to chase, then what scent will the hounds follow?" She frowned.

"The gamekeepers will have laid other scents. It could be quite the adventure."

"How clever," Hope mused. "The whole point is a good ride, after all."

The Duke had a famous string of hunters and was able to provide mounts for most of the guests, supplemented by the Cunningham stables.

Hope had never been on a proper hunter, and she was eager to make the most of the opportunity.

"This is Pegasus, miss," the groom said as he brought the beautiful chestnut forward. His bearing and disposition indicated he would be a lovely companion for the day. "Hallo, Pegasus. You look a marvellous beast," she said as she held her palm upright to offer the pieces of apple she had purloined for him, then stroked his neck. Pegasus nickered in response as he eagerly chewed the apple.

Brosner assisted her into the saddle and adjusted her stirrup and girth before mounting beside her as she smoothed her skirts. They moved their mounts to where the others were waiting.

The hounds were barely held in check by the whippers-in, baying and circling, ready to be off.

The Duke led at the front, as Master, when the horn sounded and they set off. They fell in behind, Patience paired with Montford, and Max with Caroline. Joy and Lady Susan were keeping pace right behind the Duke.

It was hard to tell what was going on from her position, so she simply enjoyed the chase. And a chase it was. The hounds ran forward, noses down, communicating with their howls and bays. The gamekeepers must have had a time laying the scents as they zigzagged across the open field to begin.

It seemed as though they ran for a mile across the home farm before the hounds thought they had something. Hope watched as they set up an unholy howl and surrounded the covert where they had their false quarry cornered. After being rewarded for their good work, the hounds then took off through the forest on a winding path, up and down, until they came to another covert.

Hope noticed the whipper-in rewarded them with scraps of meat thrown on the ground before calling them away with his horn and back down towards the river. They continued in this vein for mile after mile, the Duke still pressing on, his cheeks flushed from the exertion. It was hard not to be affected by his enthusiasm.

They broke for the morning at the fishing pool to let the horses rest and drink. A small repast had been prepared for them with sandwiches, meat pies, fruits and ale.

Hope was covered in mud and feeling glorious, if a little saddle sore. It was easy to forget and minimize her troubles amongst the exercise and camaraderie of the group.

MAX HAD to confess the ride to hounds had been a good idea. His father was happier than he had seen him in years, and perhaps that was from knowing his time was limited.

Even Max was having fun on the ride, despite watching Brosner fawn over Hope.

Max kept trying to remind himself that he had no right to feel jealous when he himself was considering other ladies as his potential bride.

Lady Caroline was painfully shy, and once they began riding, he no longer had to try to converse but enjoy the chase—except she was timid, even in her riding. He had hoped her personality would not have carried over to her horsemanship, although to be fair, the hunt was very different from a normal course. You had to go at the hounds' pace and take whatever came at you—fences, hedges, or even water. Not everyone liked the danger or unpredictability.

It looked as if the Whitford ladies were enjoying themselves, at least. He had never doubted they would be game for the sport.

Max would have to think of another way to draw Miss Montford out. Like most timid people, he felt once she was comfortable with him she would lose her bashfulness. Maybe Monty would have some suggestions.

They were at the back of the field, and he found himself trying to find ways around every obstacle yet keep up with the others. When they finally stopped for a rest, he could only feel relief, and even wondered if she might wish to retire from the field for the day.

How uncharitable he was. Did it matter if his bride was a mediocre horsewoman?

They pulled to a stop, and Max looked up to see Freddy and Monty's looks of pity. They drew alongside the rest of the group of their friends and dismounted. Waiting grooms led their horses to drink.

"You are riding like a slug-a-bed, Caroline," Monty scolded. "You should change partners so Rotham can properly enjoy the chase."

"I told you I could not do this," she said quietly, while her cheeks flushed with embarrassment.

"I am enjoying myself, Monty." Rotham felt for her, even though he been thinking the same thing. If Monty had mentioned his sister did not enjoy riding, he never would have asked her to join the hunt! He could berate him later.

"I am growing tired. We must have covered ten miles already," Diana said. "Perhaps Miss Montford would like to return to the house with me?"

Miss Montford looked relieved and grateful at the suggestion. He did feel for her and wondered why Monty had embarrassed his sister like that.

"I did not realize you did not care for hunting, Miss Montford. You need not feel uncomfortable in saying so."

"Thank you, my lord. I like riding, but had a bad fall over a hedge when I was young and never really took to it again. Monty thinks it is time I conquered my fear."

Max thought if she had not conquered it yet, she was unlikely to do so now.

That made him think of Joy's recent accident, and made him wonder how she was doing. He'd been surprised to see her out on the field this morning. However, she was as pluck to the backbone as any fellow he'd ever met, so she must be on the mend to be hanging on the coat-tails of the avid hunters in the group.

She was with his niece, Susan, right next to the Duke, laughing and eating. What a relief she was not further harmed by her illness!

With his partner gone for the day, Max could breathe a little easier —that was until he saw Brosner smiling down at Hope with undisguised admiration. Max finally knew what possessiveness could do to a temper. He'd never burned with so much envy.

He had to put an end to this once and for all. Hope was who he wanted and his mother would have to accept it. The Duke could stand up to the Duchess in this. Diana was right. Max's happiness was worth something and what Hope did not know, she could learn. And what she did not wish to do, Max could have his secretary do.

Now, if he could but be so certain Hope would have him. The way she was looking at Brosner, he was no longer confident. His friends would say it was about time he was brought down a peg or two. What they didn't know was Max had few delusions about being wanted for anything other than his title and position. Brosner's title was almost the same as his own, but he did not think Hope cared for that. If anything, it was a deterrent. Perhaps that was why Max had been able to let down his guard in Hope's company and be friends.

He finished his egg sandwich and washed it down with a jug of ale as he contemplated where to go from here. The fact was, he had made up his mind but he did not want his mother to know until it was a *fait accompli*. He feared his mother would become unhinged and do something to harm Hope. Not physically, of course, but he would not put it past her Grace to ruin Hope in Society.

Max intended to have every last detail planned, with his father's blessing, once he was assured Hope returned his affections.

Having decided, he felt a heavy weight lift from his shoulders. If only Diana hadn't left, he could share his decision with someone. However, he would not for the world have Miss Montford back as his partner that afternoon, so he would speak with his sister later.

Max walked over to where Hope was standing with her sisters and their friends and smiled at her.

"Your father is in his element," Hope said, looking over at the Duke.

"His hounds and his hunters have always been his favourites," Max said ruefully.

"He did not pass that love on to you? It appeared as though you were born in the saddle."

Max inclined his head. "Oh, I enjoy the chase, but as a sport, not a way of life."

Hope laughed, then suddenly the hairs on the back of his neck stood up for a second before he saw the flash of a pistol. He yelled as a crack sounded and reached out to pull Hope behind him while simultaneously trying to duck.

He felt something graze his arm and prayed that was the end of it.

"Are you hurt?" He looked down at Hope.

"What happened?" she asked, her big blue eyes wide and dazed.

"Someone was shooting, I am afraid. Hopefully, no one was harmed."

"Were you hit, Rotham?" Brosner asked. "It looks as though you have a tear in your coat."

"I think I was grazed. 'Tis but a scratch. Everyone else is unharmed?"

They looked around. "Who would have been shooting? All of the gamekeepers knew we would be hunting and it would be too dangerous."

"It must have been a poacher," Brosner said reasonably. "Perhaps you should have your arm bound."

It looked as though most of the men and keepers had taken off to look for the offender, to prevent anyone else being harmed.

Max realized Hope was still in his arms as she began to shake. "Are you quite well, Miss Whitford?"

Pulling back to look at her, he saw blood trickling down her neck. "Hope? Are you hurt?"

"I do not know. I feel a little strange."

He untied her bonnet and discovered the bullet had grazed the side of her head. It would have killed her if she hadn't moved.

CHAPTER 11

*H*ope was scooped up into Rotham's arms before she knew what was happening. She was dizzy, but she did not think she had fainted. It was just the shock of it all.

"You! Ride for the doctor at once and send him to the house!" Rotham barked at one of the grooms.

"You do not need to carry me," she protested weakly.

"You will be examined by Dr. Cafferty at once. When he says I have nothing to fear, then I will stop worrying."

Hope would have smiled at his protectiveness if her head did not hurt so much. A tight bandage had been wound around her temple, so she must look ridiculous, as well. At the moment, she was too tired to care.

"Brosner, help me lift her into the back of this cart," she heard Rotham order.

She was passed to a different set of hands and carefully lowered onto the bed of the vehicle. Then Rotham's arms were around her again. "Drive slowly. I do not want her to be jostled."

"Why is she losing so much blood?" Grace asked. "It does not look to be deep."

"It must have hit an artery," Patience answered.

"We must go at once," Rotham said. "We will meet you back at the house," he said to her sisters as they moved back.

The cart moved forward and Hope decided it was more comfortable to close her eyes and rest against Rotham than stay awake and endure the pain. When she woke again, she was being carried up the stairs into the house.

"Perhaps the blue drawing room, my lord?" the butler suggested. "It has been made ready for the Duke to use if needed."

Rotham placed her gently on a sofa, and her sisters soon crowded into the room to wait with her for the doctor's arrival.

Slightly dizzy, she tried to sit up and feel her head. She did not think she had been gravely injured.

"What are you doing?" Rotham asked.

"I am attempting to assess my head. I do not need everyone fussing over me." The last thing she wanted was to draw more attention to herself! Not that she could help being shot. If it had been an accident, then she had been very lucky.

"How is your arm, Rotham?" Grace asked.

Guiltily, he met Hope's gaze.

"Oh, yes. I forgot you were also hit! You had no business carrying me so!"

"After the bullet hit him, it lodged in your bonnet!" Grace said, holding up the evidence.

Hope felt a wave of nausea at the realization of how close she had been to a worse fate, and began to tremble.

Rotham attempted to soothe her, and covered her with a blanket.

Dr. Cafferty arrived shortly thereafter and stopped with surprise when he saw he had different patients. "My lord, I thought I had been called here for Miss Joy. What has happened?"

"A stray bullet from a poacher scratched my arm and then hit Miss Whitford. The bonnet and my arm seem to have slowed the trajectory a little."

The doctor set down his bag on a nearby table, then sat beside Hope on the sofa. He removed the bandage and surveyed the damage. "The bleeding has slowed. I do not think there will be much of a scar as long as the wound does not fester. The injury was not far above her eye, near her temple, as you can see. You are a very fortunate young lady. Half an inch to the left, and it could have gone into your brain."

Hope sat still, feeling numb, while the doctor cleaned and redressed the wound before standing and turning to Rotham.

"Now, let me have a look at your arm, my lord."

"I need nothing. 'Tis but a scratch."

"I will be the judge of that. Scratches can also fester. I will look now."

Hope was mildly amused at the doctor's tone with Rotham. Even though the doctor was half a head shorter than his lordship, he appeared to be looking down at him. He had probably been the family physician since before Rotham was born. They went to a different room and Hope's sisters crowded around her.

"Do you think someone tried to shoot Rotham on purpose?" Patience asked, sitting beside her on the sofa and taking her hand.

"Why would anyone wish to kill him? We should not let our imaginations carry us to nonsensical places. It could have as easily been intended for me, if that is the reasoning."

"I should not have said anything," Patience said repentantly.

"The notes are putting me on edge, as well. But none of them have threatened my life."

"Besides, I do not think anyone would be so bold as to try to shoot you with so many people nearby," Grace reasoned. "'Twould be very risky."

"I do not wish to speak about it anymore." Hope found that she had already been dwelling on the uneasy feeling and if she thought someone was now trying to kill her, it would make her suspicious beyond measure.

"Are you in pain?"

"Only a little, now."

"You should rest. We will escort you upstairs."

"The doctor did not say I needed to go to bed!" The last thing she wanted was to be alone with her thoughts.

"Very well, what do you wish to do? It will still be a few hours before the hunt is finished, I suspect."

"Perhaps we may join the other ladies?" Grace suggested.

"I think reading in the bath house might be more restful," Patience suggested as an alternative. "I know I am a bit chafed and sore from all of the jumping."

"And I would like to continue with the second volume of my book," Grace agreed.

Hope did not think she felt like reading, but she would never admit as much. She loved the bath house and could sit there for hours. As Hope began to stand, they could hear a commotion in the entrance hall.

"It sounds as though the hunters are returning," Grace remarked.

"If you would rather go and see your friends, I do not mind. I can keep myself company," Hope said.

Before they could hurry out of the room to see, a visitor appeared in the doorway.

"Faith!" they all exclaimed at once.

Grace was first to throw her arms around their beloved sister, followed by Patience. Hope remained on the sofa, filled with happiness at Faith's return.

Faith caught Hope's gaze. "What has happened? Lord Brosner said you and Rotham had been shot?" Faith asked as she came over to sit beside Hope and gave her a hug.

"Thankfully, the bullet lodged in my bonnet. The doctor says there will be no long-term effects."

"How could that have even happened?"

"A poacher is what they believe. They were searching for him as we left to bring Hope to the house," Patience explained.

"Well, thank the heavens nothing worse happened."

"I am so glad you are here," Hope said, suddenly feeling the urge to cry. She batted away the tears that threatened.

"Westwood received Rotham's note and thought it was best if we were here," Faith said. "Is something else wrong? Not that being shot isn't enough to bring anyone to tears."

Hope's throat was tight, and she gently shook her head, which made her wince. How could she explain?

Patience walked over and closed the door. "Someone has been sending her notes," she said quietly. "Not threatening, but not quite admiring either."

"Like compliments laced with warnings," Hope clarified. "I can see no reasoning for them."

Faith furrowed her brow. "I can see why you would be disconcerted. We are here now and will resolve everything."

Hope prayed Faith was right. She certainly felt better having her near.

"Please let us talk about something more pleasant. I want to hear all about Paris!"

Faith smiled. "Paris was similar to London, but still very different. There were cafés where ladies could go, and the shops were divine. My favourite part—I think—was simply walking around the city. There were artists painting on many of the street corners, and you could stroll along the river or take a leisure boat from one end of the city to the other. We dined with Wellington a couple of times. I was surprised at the English presence there again after the war. We will have to take you there soon."

"How soon?" Hope asked. "Because at this moment, it is very appealing."

Her sister laughed. "I will speak to Westwood about it."

MAX WANTED SOMEONE'S BLOOD. As soon as Dr. Cafferty had left, he was on the brink of setting out to join the hunt for the gunman when Westwood arrived. He was just trying to shirk into his coat.

"What has happened?" Westwood stopped at the threshold to the study, a scene of some disorder, having been where Dr. Cafferty had put a plaster on Max's arm.

"Dom! I am so glad you have come. Is your lady wife with you?" Max walked over and shook his best friend's hand.

"She is looking for her sisters. We passed Brosner on the way in and he broke the news that the two of you had been shot."

"Unfortunately, yes." Max proceeded to fill him in on the narrow escape he and Hope had just had.

"You are sure the shot came from a poacher?"

"I cannot think why anyone would wish to kill me or Miss Whitford! The others went to investigate. Hopefully, they will find the culprit and then we will know for certain. I was just on my way back to the field to see if I could help discover anything."

"I will go with you."

They proceeded to the front drive then climbed into the cart that had brought Hope and him back to the house.

"Shall I drive?" Westwood asked.

"I will assume you are teasing. The day I cannot drive the cart with a scratch on my arm is the day you have permission to shoot me yourself. How is married life?" Max changed the subject.

"Better than I could have imagined," Westwood answered. "However, I do not think I would have been in the right case any sooner or with anyone else."

"There is a reason for the house party, Dom. I told you my father was ill, but you have not seen him yet. He is dying."

"What has happened?" he asked.

"A wasting disease, apparently. He is weak and frail, Dom. Although he wanted to hunt, so hunting we have given him," Max said fondly. "The old boy is enjoying himself greatly."

"If I was dying, I would make the most of my time left."

"I wanted to prepare you. I did not have that luxury." Dominic had come home from school with Max on occasion, and had hunted with the Duke.

"It is hard to imagine him as anything other than a bear," Westwood reflected.

Max laughed at the apt analogy as he guided the cart along a narrow path to the watering pool.

"Father would like to see me wed, Dom. I have asked a few ladies here to see who would suit."

Westwood turned and stared at him. "What of Hope?"

Max worked his jaw as he decided how to answer. "The Duchess does not approve. That is the kind of way of expressing it. She as good as announced my betrothal to Miss Cunningham at your wedding breakfast."

Westwood whistled.

"Then she sent the announcements to the papers. It was no small feat to prevent that from going to print."

"I can only imagine." His friend groaned.

"Had the Duke not supported me in allowing me to choose my own bride, I would have been disinherited, according to her Grace."

"Help me to understand, then," Westwood said slowly. "Are you or are you not allowed to choose your bride? Because if you have no intention of offering for Hope, why would you bring her here to watch you choose someone else when you know good and well she has a tendre for you? As her guardian, I must object to such usage."

"Indeed, it was badly done of me. I can see that now," Max admitted. "I thought to reassure myself, I suppose. I had not fairly looked at anyone else and thought to see how she would handle the situation. I also hoped my mother would change her mind."

"And what has your conclusion been? Or are you still assaying ladies?"

Max did not miss his friend's sardonic tone. "There is no one else who suits me so well, and you know it as well as I."

"Who are these other paragons you thought might suit?" Westwood asked, clearly wholly amused by the state of affairs.

Max began to regale him with his experiences with Lady Alice, Lady Agatha, Lady Matilda, and Lady Caroline.

Westwood was crying with laughter when Max described the archery lesson and Lady Agatha's attempt to throw herself all over him.

"Is she not the fusby-faced one?" Westwood asked, which made Max laugh.

By that time, they had reached those guests who were hunting; there were still other people gathered about the bank. Max set the brake on the cart and looked at his friend. "Hope is the lady I want, but what am I to do about her Grace?"

"The Duchess can accept it graciously, or accept a life apart from you. Your father will soon be gone, and he was never good at taking your part, anyway."

That much was true.

A blow on the horns signalled that hounds and horses were coming. The Duke flew by on his steed, his cheeks pink from exertion and happiness.

"That was the Duke?" Westwood asked, shaking his head with disbelief that the Duke was still upright in the saddle.

"I warned you. It looks as though they have resumed the hunt," Max said as the whirl of hounds and horses passed them. "Does this mean they did not find anything? Or did they find a poacher and resolve the danger?"

Montford, Carew, and Cunningham saw Max and Westwood and pulled up beside the cart.

"Well met, Westwood!" Freddy greeted with his usual cheer.

"Any news?" Max asked, impatient for word. "Why is the hunt continuing?"

"It did not seem as though there was further risk," Carew explained.

"No sign of a poacher," Montford said. "No traps or anything left behind in a hurry."

"And no footprints in the rocky path," Freddy added. "We did find a feather," he continued, holding up a feather of an unnaturally dyed red colour.

"That could only have come from one place," Max said.

"A lady's bonnet," Westwood confirmed.

"Which does not necessarily mean the hand on the gun was that of a lady. Any number of ladies were wearing feathers in their hats this morning," Montford pointed out.

"Where was this found?"

"Come, I will show you." They climbed up the small, nearby ridge to a well-hidden spot behind some trees. It would have been a perfect place to watch, wait, and take aim.

No one said what they must all be thinking. If a lady's feather had landed there accidentally, it would have had to have been carried there by a bird or by strong winds, and it was an unusually still day.

"Too bad the hounds cannot hunt without a scent," Westwood reflected.

"I think this needs to remain between us for now," Max said thoughtfully.

"We will return to the group and take note of the headdresses worn by the ladies on the hunt, though I cannot recall any of them leaving the group," Carew suggested.

"My sister escorted Miss Montford away early, though neither of them would have had time to return and do such a thing. Moreover, they were together," Max said as he pondered.

"So that eliminates the two of them. The Whitford sisters were with us for the entire time, as well," Freddy said.

"The only other ladies were Miss Joy, Lady Susan, and Lady Claudia. I cannot fathom any of them being the culprit, but by all means, for the sake of due process, let us go and see what colours their riding hats bear," Montford said, turning his horse to follow the pack.

After their friends had gone, Max turned to Westwood. "That leaves you and me to track the movements of the other ladies who did not hunt."

Max turned the horse and cart around and began to drive back down the path to the house.

"It will raise suspicion if we begin questioning everyone's whereabouts this morning," Westwood said after some minutes.

"We must be subtle, of course. Once we see who is where when we arrive, we can ask someone we trust—your mother, for instance."

"Very well," Westwood agreed.

It so happened, after they had left the cart with a groom and returned to the house, that many of the remaining ladies were gathered in the orangery, having tea. "There is your mother, over by the statue of Neptune," Max remarked softly.

Westwood nodded and headed across to speak with his mother, who was already walking towards them, delighted to see her son. As Westwood led her out of the orangery, Max quickly scanned the room. There was no sign of Lady Matilda, but to be fair, none of the younger set of ladies was in the room. Max saw his mother's enquiring gaze, but did not go to her. He greeted a few of the matrons who were close by, then decided to join Westwood.

"I did not look for you to return before another fortnight at the very earliest!" the Dowager was exclaiming.

As Max approached, Westwood was already asking his mother how their day had been. Max made a bow and suggested they remove to his study.

"The morning has been pleasant. We have been making blankets for the parish church all morning."

They entered Max's study and Westwood led his mother to the sofa. She was still smiling at the surprise of seeing her son. "Where is Faith?" she asked.

"She is with Hope. There was a mishap during the hunt, and she and Rotham were grazed by a stray bullet."

The Dowager blinked a few times. "Is she badly harmed? I will go to her at once!" She began to rise, but Westwood stayed her with his hand.

"Thankfully, it was not deep. Rotham's arm was grazed, and Hope was hit in the forehead."

She gasped.

"But the doctor has already been here and attended her. He says there will be no lasting damage."

"Who would have been shooting during a hunt?"

"That is precisely what we would like to know. We are trying to account for everyone this morning who was not on the hunt. Do you think you could tell us who was with you all morning?"

As Max suspected, as far as she could remember, the matrons had been present the entire morning—with the exception of the occasional visit to the retiring room.

"What of the younger ladies?" Westwood asked.

"Why, I believe they went on a ride to the Cunningham estate to visit the new puppies."

Max and Westwood exchanged glances over her head.

"Thank you, Mother. We must look into a few more things, but I will see you again at dinner."

"Where is Hope? I will go to her now," she insisted.

They took the Dowager to the blue drawing room where Hope was sitting with her sisters, then headed towards the stables. As luck would have it, the young ladies were walking back to the house at the same time, including Lady Matilda—wearing a jaunty riding hat with unnaturally dyed red feathers.

CHAPTER 12

As she readied for bed that night, Hope felt much more at peace now that Faith and Westwood were there. They had moved into the chambers adjacent to hers, so there was a sense of security in knowing they were so close.

Hope climbed into bed, thinking about her prospects. There was excitement among the young ladies, with a few of their soldiering friends set to arrive the next day, and Hope tried to convince herself to be excited and even look for a potential husband amongst them. Brosner had been very attentive, so she had not given up all for lost as options other than Lord Rotham.

Rotham had been very attentive as well, but his care for her was simply as that of a friend, which only made things worse. Perhaps she could have a good marriage with someone like Brosner.

As she lay in bed, contemplating the posset Jenkins had left for her, there was a light knock on her door.

Hope saw her sister's face as the panel cracked open. "May I come in? I wasn't sure if you would still be awake."

"Yes, of course."

Faith entered, closing the door behind her, and then climbed on the bed next to Hope, just like old times.

"What are you doing in here? I thought you would be with Westwood."

"He is visiting with his friends, and I wanted to see how your head was feeling."

Hope reached up to touch the bandage. "It is sore to the touch, but my head is no longer throbbing, thankfully."

"I am relieved to hear it. I thought you might need to talk alone. Patience and Grace are worried about you. They said you have not been yourself lately."

It was true, but Hope did not want to make her sister feel guilty or responsible. "Naturally, I have been missing you."

"And I, you. But there is also the matter of Lord Rotham. Do you wish to tell me about it? Has something happened?"

"There is not much to tell. The Duchess loathes me and does not think I am a suitable bride for her son."

"What mother ever thinks someone good enough for their son?"

"The Dowager adores you," Hope pointed out.

"I am fortunate," Faith agreed.

"I have decided to consider other suitors. Lord Brosner has been very attentive."

"Has he indicated a desire to court you?" Faith asked.

"Not in words, no," Hope conceded.

"I only ask because Westwood says he desperately needs to marry a fortune."

"Of course he does!" Hope retorted cynically. "I finally meet someone else I think I could muddle along with, and he cannot afford to consider me."

"Have you given up all hope of Rotham?"

"It is very clear that he has brought all these ladies here to pick a bride. He has been paying each of them marked attention."

"Any one more than the others?" Faith asked, considering.

"Actually, no. I cannot say he seems to favour any one person. He has even continued to be very civil to me, but there is not the easiness that we had before." Hope fidgeted with the embroidered edge of the coverlet. "I do not want a marriage where I am considered beneath my husband in every way."

"Tell me he has never said so," Faith demanded, incredulous.

"Well, no, not he, but the fact that he is considering other ladies is enough to tell me he, too, doubts my suitability."

"Perhaps he is only considering other ladies to satisfy his mother," she countered.

"I do not know, Faith. Mayhap I am not suited to be a duchess. I have no desire for any of this." She waved her hand around. "I know I always thought I wanted a grand match, but I would be happy living a simple life in a cottage with him."

Faith took Hope's hand and squeezed it. "I understand completely. But do not give up just yet. Maybe things are not as they seem."

"I certainly doubt it. I cannot help but wonder if the notes I am receiving are because of his previous partiality for me."

"Do you think the Duchess is behind them? I gathered the men believed the culprit to be Lady Matilda."

"Did they say so?" Hope turned with surprise to look directly at Faith.

She could see the indecision on her face. "I was not supposed to say, but yes, they believe it may have been Lady Matilda."

"What else are you not telling me?"

She held up her hands. "That is all I know. I heard Westwood and Rotham talking about it. He came to our rooms to ask after you and invited Dominic downstairs for a drink. He wanted advice on whether or not to confront her."

"I do not think that is wise. Would it not provoke her further?" Hope asked.

"I know very little of her. They would cross the room whenever we were near, if you recall. Why Rotham invited them here is beyond me."

"Lord Wilton is a friend of the Duke's," Hope explained.

"It is a pity Rotham feels pressured to marry before the Duke dies."

Hope agreed completely. "If Lady Matilda is the culprit, do you think she will continue to harass me?"

"Not if they confront her, but I do not think they have enough proof to do so."

"Then we must catch her in action," Hope said determinedly.

"You would have to lay a trap and use Rotham as the bait."

"I could not ask him to risk so much. I think it would be best if I stayed away from him. If I made it clear I was no threat, then she would leave me alone."

"Who knows with someone that would stoop to these methods," Faith replied. "I do not think you should yet give up on your chances with Rotham. I know he returns your regard, even if he does not fully realize it. Even Westwood agrees."

Hope knew it, which was why it hurt so much more. If you cared for someone enough, you would not turn away from them. However, she had not been brought up to think as a Duke. Suddenly realizing something, she sat up from her reclining position against the pillows. "We have her handwriting!" She threw back the covers, climbed down from the bed and hurried over to the small escritoire in her room where she had placed the letters. Once she found them, she turned and held them up. "We must discover a way to have her write something, then we will know for certain if it matches."

"I imagine she is too clever for me to ask her for a sample," Faith said wryly.

"I meant to be sly. A parlour game, mayhap?"

"That is not a bad idea. I can suggest it to Rotham. Although she might have had someone write it for her to avoid anyone linking the notes to her."

"I would never trust another person to keep my secret if I did something clandestinely such as that," Hope said with disbelief.

"Not even me?" Faith looked hurt.

"Would you allow me to get away with something so wicked?" she countered. Then a yawn overtook her.

"Never. We can talk to Rotham in the morning. Time for bed. I should not have kept you awake so long after your accident."

"I am glad you did. Your visit has kept me from my thoughts. How I've missed you!"

"And I you." Faith pulled Hope into a hug before turning to the door. "Is this another note?" She bent over and picked up the innocuous-looking piece of paper that had come to mean fear to Hope. "Shall I open it?"

Hope nodded, whilst dreading the words.

Faith gasped then read it to her.

A lucky escape you had. Was it a warning or an accident?

"What a horrible thing to suggest, that the shot might have been intentional!"

Hope did not want to think about that. The note made it very clear it had been. "Do you think they were listening the whole time?"

"It is hard to say, but I would think the risk of being caught too great. I must show this to Westwood." Faith started towards the door, but Hope grabbed her arm.

"I do not want to stay here alone," she pleaded.

"Then put on a wrapper and we will go down together."

MAX WOULD HAVE CONFRONTED Lady Matilda at the time if Westwood had not restrained him. Instead, he had ushered Max into his own study and thrust a glass of brandy in his hands. He trusted all his friends, but Westwood was his best friend and now also Hope's brother-in-law.

"If someone has shot at Hope because of me...having seen how close I have come to losing her...I have to do something, Dom. I have to speak with Lady Matilda."

"I understand, but would it not be better to enquire if she left Miss Cunningham's sight for a time before accusing them of attempted murder over a feather? No one saw her there, and why would she do such a thing?" He shook his head. "It makes no sense. I still think it much more likely to have been an accident," Westwood said reasonably.

Max sighed heavily and leaned his head over the back of the armchair. He closed his eyes and tried to think of the best solution. He could not shake the feeling someone had deliberately shot at him or Hope. If they meant harm, would they stop at that?

There was a soft knock at the door. "Enter," he called. There, on the threshold, was Hope, standing with her sister, the new Lady Westwood. Her hair was plaited, and the bandage was still wrapped around her head. She wore a thick dressing gown that was so prim and girlish it was hard not to smile, but from the look on her face, there was nothing to smile about. He jumped out of his chair and went to her, taking her hands in his. She was shaking. "What has happened?"

Lady Westwood handed him a letter. "This has just been slipped under her door."

He took it and read it with a muttered curse.

"There have been others, my lord," Lady Westwood said.

He looked from her to Hope, and he could tell from the expression on her face that it was true. He led her to one of the sofas and sat down with her, still holding her hands.

"Tell me about them," he said gently.

She took a deep breath, then said hesitantly, "It started the day we arrived. At first, they didn't seem threatening, but then I could not be sure. This one leaves little doubt." A tear rolled down her face and Max wanted to kiss it away. He wanted to draw her into his arms and never let her go.

"Why did you not tell me?" He felt unconscionably hurt. Friends told each other these things. "I wish to see all the letters, if you please."

"I think it might be wise to post guards on that hallway, and perhaps even have the maid sleep with her at night," Westwood said, having read the note for himself.

"I think we should move her to a different room and not tell anyone," Max countered.

"Faith and I could exchange places with her. Then it would not be so obvious," Westwood suggested. "We are more likely to catch the person if they do not realize she has told us."

Max wanted to put Hope in a tower where no one else could reach her until they found out who was doing this. "How do you propose we catch her?" he asked.

"We were thinking perhaps a trap," Lady Westwood said. "If Lady Matilda is responsible, that should not be too difficult. Hope said she has already tried to seek you out once."

He ran his hand through his hair. "Yes. Do you have an idea?"

"The simplest solution would be to find a way for her to write something. If we can compare the two, then that would give us some evidence."

"We also have the feather," Westwood reminded them.

"What feather?" Hope asked.

"We found a red feather where we think the shooter was waiting."

"And Lady Matilda was wearing a red feather this morning? I confess I did not notice." She frowned, as if trying to picture her.

"Yes," he confirmed.

'Why would Lady Matilda have been wearing a riding hat if she was not hunting? Were the ladies not sewing for the parish church?" Hope asked.

"Apparently, the younger ladies rode over to the Cunningham estate to see the puppies," he explained.

"I see." She shook her head. "I have never taken Lady Matilda as a malicious person. There must be an easier way to compromise someone without removing all the competition."

"I agree, it does not quite make sense, but what other leads do we have to go on?"

"None. We cannot even say definitively that the writing is female."

"How else could we trap her? Do you suggest I wander around the estate alone?" Max asked.

Westwood chuckled.

"I wonder if it wouldn't be better to use me as the bait," Hope said quietly. "Otherwise you will never know for sure, unless she confesses."

"No. Absolutely not," Max said. "She has already proved she's willing to kill."

Hope shuddered beside him. "Why would someone want to kill me?"

"We do not know for certain that they meant to kill," Lady Westwood said softly, doubtless trying to make her feel better.

"That is true," Max agreed. "They may not have been a very good shot or even familiar with that type of gun. And I moved when I heard the shot."

She worried her lower lip with her teeth. Anything he said would hardly reassure her. He had been hurt himself; he understood how she felt. "The bullet could also have been intended for me," he pointed out.

"Except no one is writing you threatening notes."

She had him there.

"With your permission, I would like to enlist my sister's help. She will be able to have the other ladies' help in addressing invitations to the ball. That way it would not appear we were singling anyone out."

"And if someone else wrote the note, it might reveal that," Westwood agreed.

"That certainly sounds better to me than putting a target on either of us," Hope agreed.

"I will speak with Diana. Even if the invitations are done, she could say there were a few more to do."

"And I think it time we retire. I will stay with Hope tonight, then we can make arrangements to switch chambers in the morning," Lady Westwood said.

"We will escort you upstairs," Max said. "I think it is for the best."

Max reached for Hope's arm as Westwood had naturally taken his wife's, but Hope shrank back from him.

"I think it for the best if we keep our distance from one another, considering the situation."

Max felt as though he'd had a punch to the stomach.

"She's right, Rotham," Westwood said. "We will see her safely to her chambers."

As they turned to leave, he reached for the air then let his arm drop. Perhaps they were right, but just as he had decided she was the one, she pushed him away.

CHAPTER 13

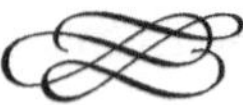

The next morning, most of the matrons were not yet down for the day so only the younger ladies were present at breakfast. It was a warm summer morning; the birds were singing and the air was fresh with the scent of the nearby rose garden. Hope woke to find Faith's maid in the room with her, but not Faith.

Hope could not bring herself to feel anything more than melancholy over the events of the previous day. She had received plenty of sympathy as a result of the accidental shooting, as they all thought it, and so thankfully no one knew her low spirits were due to what she felt was a permanent removal from Lord Rotham. It was too dangerous even to be his friend any longer.

Her energies needed to turn towards helping catch whoever wished her harm. As she went downstairs, there was excitement in the air, as some of their favourite soldiers were expected to arrive that day. Even her sisters were blooming with anticipation and more excitable than usual.

When she saw Lady Diana strolling across the terrace towards them with obvious intent, she was very glad of it.

"Good morning, ladies! If you are finished with your repast, I wish you might give me your assistance for just a few minutes. A few more invitations need to be sent out directly, and if all of you help me, it will be done in a trice!" she said to the two tables full of young ladies, in a way that made it difficult to refuse. Hope needed to learn how to do that.

There was nothing suspicious whatsoever about the request, and each of them—Lady Matilda included—copied out a few invitations to be delivered immediately.

Hope did not doubt these had already been sent out, but it was very cleverly done, and she could only be grateful.

As she observed Lady Matilda writing, she could detect nothing in her behaviour or composure that indicated any self-consciousness about showing her best script for others to see. Either she was a very cool customer, or she had nothing to do with it. Neither did she behave any differently towards Hope. Would there not be some sly glances or malice in her eyes?

As they finished each one, they handed the invitations to Lady Diana, who proceeded to sort them and place them in stacks.

"You have saved me a great deal of time, ladies. I will see these are delivered immediately!"

"Would anyone care to walk in the rose garden? It offers an excellent prospect of the front drive, I assure you," Lady Claudia said with a knowing smile.

The other young ladies giggled and happily followed Lady Claudia from the room. "Are you coming with us?" Patience turned to ask Hope.

"I think I will stay behind for now. I still have a headache," Hope explained.

Patience frowned. "Shall I stay with you?"

"No, I promise I am well. I will call for Faith if I need anything."

"I will have Mrs. Watson send up her special tisane," Lady Diana assured Patience.

Once they had left, Hope turned eagerly towards the invitations.

"Shall we take these into the study?" Lady Diana asked.

Hope hesitated, knowing *he* might be in there, but as he was involved, she assented. She followed down a corridor and a flight of stairs to the now familiar study that was primarily a masculine domain, with its dark walls and hunting trophies staring down at her.

No one was in the room and Hope breathed a sigh of relief. She could examine the writing at her leisure.

"Max should join us shortly," her ladyship said, erasing Hope's wishes. "I kept the cards arranged alphabetically so we would know whose writing was whose."

Hope took the first notes out of her pocket and laid them upon the desk. Rotham had kept the one from the evening before. It was easy to eliminate most people immediately. Hope recognized Patience's and Grace's hand without being told. It was likewise with Lady Diana and her sister, Claudia…

Which only left Vivienne Cunningham, Lady Caroline, Lady Agatha, and Lady Matilda to sort.

Miss Cunningham's writing looked as young and cheerful as she was. Miss Montford's was perfect copperplate, Lady Agatha's was more severe with bold strokes, but Lady Matilda's was extremely careless, as though she had never been rapped on the knuckles by a strict governess for poor penmanship.

"What do you think?" Lady Diana asked.

"I think none of them are even close to that on the notes," Hope said with the disappointment she felt.

"Lady Matilda's is quite untidy. Do you think it might be a deliberate ruse?" she asked.

"I suppose it could be," Hope conceded, "but it would take a great deal of skill to be so very different." She held up her sample along with the first letter for Lady Diana's inspection.

"Yes, I agree with you. Then perhaps we are circling the wrong prey?"

"What prey?" Lord Rotham asked as his tall, lean form came into the room.

Lady Diana passed over Lady Matilda's written invitation along with a note for his inspection.

"This is certainly not a match—if, indeed, it is her true penmanship. She is either very clever, or someone else wrote the note.

However, it does not entirely eliminate her. She could have bribed someone else to do it."

Hope shook her head. "I do not believe it was her. I studied her and detected no cunning in her. I think the red feather was an awful coincidence."

"If that is the case, then we are back to where we began."

"Not entirely. We have eliminated several people, and we now know that I was the intended target."

"I wish we had more to go on." Rotham paced with frustration. "I will consult with Westwood to see if we can form a plan."

Hope nodded, but all she wanted was time alone to think. There had to be somewhere she could go undetected. All of the young ladies were accounted for in the front gardens, outside the study window, and no one would know in advance of her plans as they had with the hunt. "I think I will return to my chambers and rest for a while," she said so that Rotham would let her go. Her chambers were not far down the hall from there, and they had posted footmen at either end as promised. "Thank you for your assistance in this matter."

The way he looked at her threatened to melt away her resolve, but she turned away so she would not change her mind.

"Would you like Diana to escort you?"

"It is not far, and with the footmen posted, I will do very well, thank you."

He held the door for her and she smiled slightly at him as she passed by. The door did not close behind her, so she assumed Rotham was watching her progress. Once she had turned the corner, she fled to the nearest door to escape, hoping no one had witnessed her flight. The overbearing need for space outweighed any consideration of safety.

Watching from the doorway, she saw a few people meander away from the garden towards the south lawn for games, she assumed, and took the chance to sneak past.

Patience and Grace had become best friends with Vivienne Cunningham and Lady Claudia, as had Joy with Lady Susan, and it was likely they would be occupied with their friends for most of the day. Faith was somewhere with Westwood, and Hope did not think they would miss her for a while.

She was not fit for company, with her mind whirling, and walking seemed the only way to clear her head. Besides, she needed to do something active and this beautiful estate was begging to be explored.

Thankful she had chosen her jean half-boots instead of slippers, she set off on a gravel path that headed towards the river. As she passed under the overarching pines, oaks, and black alders, the sun was blocked by the canopy of the trees and the shade from the peak.

Her situation was beginning to feel desperate, and she did not understand why someone would hate her enough to shoot at her. It had to go beyond mere jealousy…someone wanted her out of the way. Not wanting to think about it anymore, she climbed where no one would think to look for her.

She could feel her breaths coming shorter as she began to ascend the peak. It had not been her intention to climb, but she did not fear becoming lost. However, she would need to turn around in time to be back before she was missed.

As she reached the top, the wind picked up, blowing her dress and pulling her hair free from its loose pins. The sense of freedom and exhilaration were worth it. She sat for a while on a large boulder, needing the time to compose her thoughts and ask God why this was happening. He did not answer, but somehow, as she looked out over the vast vista of square fields, running water, and rocky terrain, she felt as but a speck of dust. Up there, her problems were not so significant.

Clouds began to move in, and she knew it was time to return. Faith would be visiting her room soon and would worry. Reluctantly, she rose and shook out her skirts, brushing away the dirt. She descended much more quickly, but she had only reached the bottom when a crack of thunder signalled an impending storm.

She paused, wondering if she could reach the house, when an eerie feeling of being watched made her shiver. "Impossible," she told herself. "The shooting and notes are making you fanciful! Besides, who would be out here now?"

The rain began to fall, and since the bath house was near, she sought refuge within its portals. Already soaked, she breathed a sigh of relief when she found the door unlocked.

Thrusting the door closed behind her, she leaned against it to catch her breath and was looking about to see if anyone was there when she heard the key turn in the door behind her.

"Wait! No! Someone is in here!" She beat upon the door, wishing she could see through it. Then she ran over to one of the windows, but the rain was falling too hard to make out more than distorted shapes. Fear and panic began to grip at her, and she ran back to the door to see if there was a key or any means of escape. Unfortunately there was no key to be found. Shaking with fear, Hope sank to the floor and began to cry. How long would it be until someone searched for her?

LORD WESTWOOD'S BROTHER, Major Ashley Stuart, and a few of his fellow soldiers arrived around noon, much to the delight of the house party guests.

Both Major Stuart and Captain Fielding were great favourites with the gentlemen and young ladies alike. They had both been an integral part of exposing the villain when the Whitford ladies had been in danger when they had first come to London.

In fact, Max wondered if he should not bring all the men together again to see if they could help ferret out the offender. First, though, he would consult with Westwood to see if he was considering any danger that might present. The only thing which sprang to mind was if the note was from one of them, but quickly dismissed the thought. Other than Captain Fielding, he'd known all of them since their young days at Eton and would swear to their innocence. But as Major Stuart and Captain Fielding had just arrived, neither of them could have written the notes.

The younger set was currently engrossed in a lively game of pall mall on the lawn, but he had not seen Hope again since that morning.

Perhaps it would be wise to see if Lady Westwood had visited her recently. He would prefer to do so himself, but had to respect her wishes to stay away.

As he approached, he could hear the mallets striking the balls with vigour as each player attempted to demonstrate feats of skill. Shouts of triumph or groans of disappointment echoed the spirited competitiveness of the players. Much to his amusement, he found Lord and Lady Westwood in a heated competition, so he was forced to watch the end of the game before speaking with her. He had noticed that all the Whitford sisters were fierce competitors, and it was extremely amusing to watch his equally competitive best friend being so well matched.

Of course, the Duchess would say ladies of high breeding would never be so lively, but frankly, Max wanted a wife who wasn't a dull dish.

Westwood had the last shot, and it was his to win or lose. If Max knew Westwood at all, he would knock his wife's ball out of the way to win, which is exactly what he did. He held up his hands and mallet in victory to begrudging applause from his wife.

"I suppose you have to win on occasion," she conceded in a teasing manner.

The look they exchanged was one of deep affection, and Max wanted that for himself. He wanted it with Hope.

"Rotham," Westwood greeted him when he saw him standing there.

Max smiled at him, then turned towards Lady Westwood with a bow. "A well-fought match, but every now and then he will sneak a win in."

"As long as it is not too often, sir."

"Have you seen your sister recently?"

"Why, no, I have not seen Hope at all today. When I left her room, the maid stayed with her. I was just about to go looking for her."

"I have not seen her since before noon. She was returning to her chambers to rest."

Westwood was checking his pocket watch. "It is drawing close to four."

"How quickly the time passes! Surely she will be down for tea?" Lady Westwood wondered aloud, but she was frowning. "Perhaps I should go and see."

"Take one of your sisters with you, my love. I want to speak with Rotham," Westwood said.

She nodded and hurried away, gathering Patience as she went.

"Do you think something has happened?" Westwood asked.

"Not at all, I just haven't seen her. I could hardly go and look for myself."

Westwood inclined his head. "Any success with the handwriting sample?"

"Yes and no," Max replied. "None of them matched, so it seems to eliminate the young ladies, unless one of them was drastically altering their script."

Westwood was pursing his lips in deep thought. "If not one of the young ladies, then what about the mothers? Would any of them be ambitious enough to wish Hope out of the way? You and I have both certainly had our share of attempted compromises."

"The only one I could possibly imagine in that situation would be Lady Wilton. But to shoot at Hope? And whoever fired that shot also hit me," Max felt compelled to remind him.

"I do not think we are dealing with a rational person, Max."

"I fear you are right. It makes predicting what they will do next nigh impossible."

"I think we should move inside. It looks as if rain is imminent," Westwood said, looking up.

Max followed his gaze to see dark clouds forming. They turned to walk back to the house and barely reached the steps when the skies opened in a deluge.

"Gilford, will you please let Lady Westwood know we will be in my study? I feel that is the safest choice rather than chase after them and miss them."

"Very good, my lord."

It was not long until she arrived with Patience. "She is not there! I asked the footmen on guard, and they had not seen her pass since early this morning!"

Max began to pace about the room. "How could this have happened?"

"We must not be alarmed. There could be a simple explanation," Westwood's calm was infuriating.

"I have to do something!" He felt utterly and completely desperate.

"We will find Lady Diana and our sisters, and begin discreetly searching the house," Lady Westwood said.

"Yes, that is reasonable with the weather as it is, although it came upon us quickly. I will speak to Gilford and discover if he saw her go outside or knows of her whereabouts."

"I will assist the ladies until you tell me otherwise. I will begin with my mother's maid, Jenkins," Westwood offered. "If I recall correctly, she is a veritable fount of information."

They divided up, and Max went to find the butler. "I have not seen her this day, my lord. I could enquire at the stables if you wish?"

"No, no. I will go. I need to do something, but please assist Westwood with whatever he asks in this matter."

"Of course, my lord." He was already handing Max a hat and cape. "Would you like an umbrella, my lord?"

"Yes, if Miss Whitford is caught out in the rain, she would appreciate that very much, though it might be pointless in the wind." Max set out for the stables, and the rain was coming down so hard he would not have had an easy time of it had he not known the way. If Hope was out in this, he prayed she had found some shelter. If she wandered about, she could easily become lost and with the rocky terrain and fast river, it could be dangerous.

He was drenched by the time he struggled through the stable door, but all the horses were accounted for, and Hope was nowhere to be found. None of the grooms or the stable master had seen her, nor had any of the young ladies taken a horse out that day.

After he had directed the grooms to be ready for a search of the grounds, he returned to the house, frustrated, to see if she had been found there. Instead, he found her sisters distressed and fretting.

"No one has seen her since this morning, Max," Diana said. "We are still searching the other wing, but there is no reason to believe she would have ventured there."

"I watched her round the corner from the study," he said, thinking and walking towards where he had last seen her at the same time. "Could someone have been lying in wait?"

"There is a door to the garden down the steps. Do you think she would have gone outside?" Diana asked.

"Despite knowing someone has been threatening her? Why would she do such a thing?" The thought made him incredulous.

"Hope can be stubborn. She might have gone somewhere she felt safe," Patience said.

"She barely knows the estate," Diana said in a panic.

"We rode over a great deal of it during the hunt," Patience reasoned. "Perhaps she went for a walk and is sheltering somewhere until the rain stops."

Max turned to Westwood, about to call for all available men to begin a search, when Patience had an idea.

"Has anyone looked in the bath house? If I wanted to rest, that is where I would go. Perhaps she fell asleep and was caught unawares by the storm."

"It is worth a try. I am going to look for her. If she is not there, we will gather everyone to search."

"I will go with you," Westwood said.

"No, there is no need to send you out unless necessary. It is not far. I will return soon."

A loud crack of thunder shook the house just as he readied a lantern to go out, and he and Westwood exchanged ominous glances as he set forth to find Hope.

Max could not shake the fear that whoever wished her ill was responsible for this. He had to find her before it was too late.

CHAPTER 14

$\mathcal{A}$s Hope realized no one would come out in the storm looking for her, she tried not to become panic-stricken. Yet her mind could not but wonder if the person who had locked her in was lying in wait to further harm her. It could have been an accident, she tried to tell herself, but it certainly felt deliberate considering the circumstances.

Venus looked mockingly down at her as she debated what to do. "I do not suppose you know an alternative way out, do you?" she asked the large statue. "If ever I needed an act of God, it is now." All she received was a blank stare from the marble face. "You, oh fair goddess, are a fraud."

Instead of standing there talking to carved stone, she decided to see if there was another door. One more try on the door she had entered through confirmed it was still locked.

The palpable air, heavy with the scent of citrus and moist earth would usually have been welcome, but the damp air only made her soaked clothing chill her more. The arrangement of the bath house was such that she could not simply feel her way along the walls. The cool, uneven stone beneath her fingertips contrasted starkly with the occasional brush against a leaf as she made her way around to the opposite wall, where she prayed for a window that would open. Sporadic lightning cast ghostly silhouettes of the trees, creating an eerie tapestry against the walls but not enough light for her to find a window with a latch.

Now shivering, Hope shrank to the floor and crawled her way to the alcove where she'd been so happy just two days before. It was their secret place, where she could feel slightly more safe within its confines and a little closer to Rotham. She needed to stop thinking that way about him, but for the moment, she needed anything to keep her mind from who was tormenting her.

"It is just a storm. Soon, Faith will realize you are gone and come looking for you," she reasoned with herself.

Thunder continued to rattle through the valley, shaking the portals of the marble and glass edifice. Occasional streaks and flashes of lightning would provide respite from the darkness, but mostly she was alone with her morbid thoughts. It was impossible to keep them away. There would be no peace for her as long as someone was determined on this course of destroying—or doing away with—her.

A peal of thunder reverberated through her very bones as rain lashed against the windows, its rhythm a relentless, percussive accompaniment to the storm's fury outside. How long could a storm last?

Curling into a tight ball, she closed her eyes to block out the imagined faces in the shadows. Who would want to do this to her? Hope could not give credibility to someone like Lady Matilda. Smaller tricks, yes, but there was too much cunning involved. She'd seen all of the young ladies playing pall mall as she'd left for her walk. Perhaps they could have made their excuses, but with suspicions heightened, it would have been quite obvious. Something told Hope that the plot against her was more sophisticated, and that it had to be someone with an intimate knowledge of Davenmere. Who else could have shot at them and then made their escape?

The thought was too awful to allow her mind to continue down that path. The storm would be over soon, and someone would realize she was missing by dinnertime, surely. She closed her eyes and drifted into a light dream of when Rotham had still been attainable.

"Hope? Hope?" A voice called to her distant state of awareness.

She stirred and sat up; warm hands gathered her into a pair of firm arms and a cape encircled her for warmth.

"Hope, my love. I am here. You are chilled!"

"Rotham? Thank God," she said through chattering teeth, which was as much from nerves as the cold.

"You should have told someone where you were going. I have been worried beyond enduring. I was about to gather a search party." His hands were rubbing up and down her arms, then chafing at her hands.

"W-wa-was walking. C-c-caught in the storm. Then someone locked the door."

By the dim light of his lantern, she caught a confused look from Rotham. "But it was not locked, my dear."

"I heard the key turn in the lock. And I tried the door!" she insisted.

"I have no key, and I walked straight in."

Hope began to argue, but he hushed her with a fingertip on her lips.

"We can sort that out later. We must get you back to the house and warm again."

Warm sounded lovely, but she knew the door had been locked. She had tried it twice and knew she was not imagining it.

Some of the sensation was beginning to return to her as he continued to soothe her with his hands. He swept some of the wet hair back from her face and tenderly placed as kiss on her forehead.

"I will take you back to the house now and never let you out of my sight again," he murmured.

They were the words she had so desperately longed to hear. She allowed herself to nestle against his shoulder and breathed in his musky scent, mixed with rain, just one more time.

"Hope, if anything ever happened to you…" His voice trailed off. He held her face gently and looked deep into her eyes. His face moved towards hers, and he gently brushed his lips across hers.

A fluttering sensation beat rapidly within her chest as she leaned forward for more. For a few brief moments, all of her troubles melted away into the sensation of his kiss. Nothing existed but the two of them and the magical feeling between them. Perhaps she was dreaming, but she wanted to be closer to him as he deepened the kiss. When he pulled his lips from hers, he showered her face with tender caresses before returning to her lips for more.

"No, stop. This cannot be," she said, as much to herself as to him.

"Hope, I want to be with you. Forever. Do you understand what I am saying to you?"

She shook her head. "It is impossible," she whispered, though doubted he could hear her over the storm. It was a shame that what had finally brought them together was also tearing them apart.

"Nothing is impossible if we are both determined to make it so." He looked at her long and hard and must have seen resignation or resolve there. "This is not the time to speak of it. Come, let us get you back to the house and warm."

He gathered her into his arms, carefully draping the cape over them both as much as possible.

"Can you hold the umbrella and the lantern?" he asked.

She nodded and noticed as he pushed the door open easily that there could have been no mistaking it for being hard to open.

As he hurried them through the blowing rain back to the house, her tears mixed with the drops that hit her face despite the umbrella, which she struggled to hold close against the wind.

He ushered her in through the side door she had slipped out of earlier, then up the stairs to his study, where Westwood and her sisters were waiting for her.

"You can put me down now," she told him.

The look on his face said that he would gladly hold her forever, but he did as she wished.

"Thank God!" Faith said as she came towards her. "Come. A warm bath awaits you, and you can tell me what happened."

She turned and looked back at Rotham, willing him to believe her, yet unable to utter pleas for the tightness in her throat.

~

MAX STOOD in the drawing room, speaking to Westwood whilst waiting for the dinner guests to assemble and watching the door anxiously to see if Hope would come down.

"Do you believe someone really locked her in?" Westwood asked. "Or do you think she perhaps became panic-stricken?"

"If she was anxious, then why go out alone?" Max countered.

"According to Faith, Hope has to walk to reflect when something is troubling her. It was daylight, and she thought everyone was accounted for and would not see her slip away."

"It was still a risk I would not have had her take. All I can say is, that if someone locked the door, then they are deliberately playing with her mind, because it was unlocked when I tried it," Max said with a shake of his head.

Westwood held a palm upward. "Faith thinks it for the best if we do not tell anyone. She was trying to convince Hope to come down to dinner and behave as though nothing has happened."

Max disagreed. He wanted her kept out of harm's way until he had personally questioned everyone in the household, with whatever means necessary to wring information out of them. He would ask Major Stuart and Captain Fielding to help with whatever techniques they'd learned in the army.

"The more unaffected she appears, the more it should draw our person out," Westwood continued calmly, whilst Max's blood was still simmering. Finding her shaking and scared brought out the protective beast within him, and he wanted to conquer all predators from ever harming her again. Max saw his mother approaching, and he unconsciously clenched his fists. She looked cold and rigid in dove grey, her frosty expression enhanced by the severity of her tight chignon.

"At ease, soldier," Westwood said quietly next to him. "Do I stay for support or leave you?"

Westwood knew more than anyone of the Duchess' unkind nature. He was the only one he'd confided in, as a fellow boarder, when she'd been particularly overbearing. Yet nothing compared to her behaviour with respect to his future bride. They bowed as she approached.

"Westwood, do your bride and her sister intend to join us for dinner?"

"They should be here momentarily, ma'am."

Max watched his mother's face closely. "Did Diana send you over here to enquire?" he asked, knowing it would irritate her that he'd reminded her of her place. She'd been desperately trying to prove she was still the hostess.

"I was referring to Miss Whitford's accident the day prior. I did not know if she was indisposed."

Max would like to think his mother had asked for charitable reasons, but more likely she was hoping her wound would fester.

"She is well, I thank you," Westwood said. "Here they are now, your Grace. You may enquire after her health yourself."

Max turned to see for himself if Hope evidenced any ill effects from her adventure, but she looked as radiant as ever. She wore a pale rose silk gown with delicate embroidery over the bodice and hem. She had even reduced the bandage around her head, which was discreetly covered by curls and a riband.

Lady Westwood and Miss Whitford sank into curtsies. "Your Grace, my lords," they said, and Max noticed Hope stopped her gaze in the region of his neckcloth. Why would she not look at him? Knowing the Duchess' shrewd eyes were watching every moment, he decided to hold nothing back.

"My mother was just enquiring after your health, Miss Whitford. Are you recovering well from your injury?"

Hope smiled with politeness and looked towards the Duchess, who, up close, was seething beneath the icy veneer.

"How kind of you, your Grace. As you can see, 'tis but a scratch, to borrow the phrase from Lord Rotham."

"I was not aware the language of the stables was encouraged in your drawing room, Rotham," the Duchess replied with icy scorn before deliberately turning her back on Hope.

They were saved by Gilford announcing dinner.

"May I have the pleasure of escorting you into dinner?" Max asked, loudly enough the Duchess could not but overhear.

He saw her spine stiffen in his periphery, but he did not give her the satisfaction of letting her show him her censure. How she would protest when she knew Hope was his choice! He would do everything in his power to shield his bride when the time came. First, however, they had to ferret out who was harassing her.

Max fully intended to show everyone exactly where Hope stood in his affections with actions, if not yet words. Words would come soon enough. But he knew he also had to prove himself to her first.

If there was surprise that he was escorting Miss Whitford into dinner, no one said anything, though he could sense his mother shooting daggers at him behind his back. He walked her towards the head of the table and pulled out the chair for her to be seated next to the Duke.

"What is this?" she whispered.

"His Grace has requested your company this evening."

"But Rotham, it will only draw unwanted attention to me!" she protested in a quiet voice.

"Smile, my dear. This will show them you are protected by the Duke," he said, as he gently sat her in the chair, then pushed it forward.

When the ladies were all seated, the men joined them. His father was looking a little fatigued, but he flashed Hope a wide smile. "Remind me to thank whoever made the seating arrangements tonight." He winked at her.

Gus was on her other side and Lady Conway was directly across. Max was only three seats down and across the table, but he knew his brother and father would put her at ease. He avoided looking at the Duchess from the other end of the table. Her displeasure was palpable.

Diana had seated herself close to the Duchess, no doubt to try to defuse her ire, bless his sister. She had even asked the kitchens to prepare her Grace's favourite dishes of crab bisque and lobster patties that night so there would be less to criticize.

"Devilish bad luck someone shooting so close to the hunt. I trust your head is mending well?" Max heard his father ask Hope.

"Yes, your Grace. Dr. Cafferty even thinks I will not have much of a scar."

The Duke waved his hand in the air. "Your beauty could withstand many such marks and not be tarnished."

Hope blushed charmingly. "You flatter me, your Grace."

Max realized he was ignoring his dinner partner and forced his eyes from Hope. Thankfully, with the addition of the soldiers, conversation was more animated than it had been the previous nights.

He noticed that Colonel Renforth, one of the visiting officers, was a handsome, jovial fellow who was doing a surprising job of charming the Duchess. Anything to keep her mind away from Max and Hope, her undutiful son mused thankfully.

"It was good of you to invite the soldiers here, my lord," Miss Patience said when it was her turn to speak with him.

"I must confess, it was not my idea. Major Stuart hinted they would be in the neighbourhood. He knows he always has an open invitation."

"Then I must thank you for that," she said with a twinkle in her eye.

"Was the party so very dull without them?" he teased.

"Only for those with a partiality for a gentleman in uniform."

"In my experience, that includes most females," he said, with a wry twist of his lips.

"Guilty as charged," she said, with an unrepentant smile.

They ceased talking while the next course was placed before them.

"Thank you for finding Hope," she said quietly once their plates were full again. "She was rather shaken by the incident."

He nodded. "I am thankful you knew where to look."

"We have to discover who is doing this to her. Otherwise, I fear we may soon have to leave."

"Do you fear for her safety?" Max was appalled at the thought, even though it was well justified, he realized.

"Frankly, I do. The notes appear to be more…" she searched for the right word, "…aggressive each time, and it seems to me that there are too many accidents occurring to be coincidence."

"The only accident was the shooting," he said thoughtfully.

She leaned closer and kept her voice low. "What about the chocolate that made Joy ill? Perhaps it was adulterated and intended for Hope. Then someone locking her in the bath house for a time? Perhaps they did not intend her harm, but it certainly shook her spirits. Then the notes…" She gestured with her hands. "It seems too coincidental to me."

Max frowned. "I hope you are wrong, but we must keep her in sight at all times. Hopefully, you and your sisters can convince her not to wander off again."

"I do not think it will take any convincing after today."

Max took a bite of a lobster patty and chewed thoughtfully. If Patience was right, then it was worse than he'd imagined. What would they try to do to Hope next? And why?

CHAPTER 15

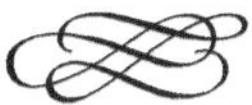

Faith would not let Hope out of her sight unless she was with someone else. In most ways it was comforting, but knowing that someone was still watching her every move was enough to have her running mad. Perhaps that was the intention.

The house had been a hive of activity as they made ready for the ball that night. The aromas of baking bread and roasting meat wafted through the mansion as the kitchens prepared for both dinner and supper. The arrangement of flowers, placing of fresh candles in the fixtures, and the setting out of chairs was attended to by dozens of servants, while the musicians arrived and saw to tuning their instruments.

The ladies hummed with anticipation and retired early to their chambers to prepare their toilettes for the evening.

Hope should have been excited, but most of her day had been spent observing everyone of the party, and wondering who wished her harm. After the particular attention she'd been paid the night before, she expected a fresh, scathing note to be awaiting her that morning. None had yet come. The waiting for it was almost worse. She could not imagine they would simply stop.

Jenkins took care in curling her hair and covering up the bandage from her healing gunshot wound. It still seemed fantastical to think she'd been shot at. In continuing with the tradition of each sister wearing certain colours, Jenkins had selected a jonquil silk with a darker bodice and golden lace over-slip and had set out gold earrings and a necklace to match.

"You look a treat, miss," the maid said when she surveyed her handiwork.

"Thank you, Jenkins. I only wish I felt a treat." Hope decided she might as well see what the maid knew. She was so desperate for a resolution. "Jenkins."

"Yes, miss?"

"I do not know how much your mistress is taking you into her confidence, but someone has been sending me unsigned notes, and I have been involved in several incidents which have appeared to be accidents, but feel very intentional. Have you noticed anything out of the ordinary at all?"

Her round, rosy face brightened with excitement at getting to share some gossip. "His lordship did ask me a few things which made me wonder," she admitted. "And then there were the footmen stationed at either end of the hall."

"Have they seen anything?"

"If they have, they haven't told me, but I did hear the Duchess asking them to report any unusual activity directly to her, when she did not know I was nearby."

"Does she think to catch me doing something clandestine?"

"I could not say, miss, but she is a cold one." The maid shivered dramatically.

There was a knock on her door, and Faith looked inside. "May we come in?"

"Of course," Hope said, and was a bit surprised when her sister's husband followed her inside and closed the door. Faith was looking radiant in a blue net gown with capped sleeves over a cream-coloured slip trimmed with gauze roses around the hem. Hope had to admit that marriage suited her sister very well.

"How are you feeling?" Faith asked in her motherly way.

"As well as can be expected," Hope admitted.

"You look very elegant," Westwood said with a fond smile. "Forgive the intrusion, but I wanted to know how I can help you. As you know, I have a band of friends who will step in at the lift of your finger."

Hope smiled with sadness. "Why is it that we are always in need of rescue, Faith?" she asked her sister, recalling Westwood's friends coming to their rescue once before.

"You are a threat to someone," Westwood answered. "I am convinced this is all the work of a female. This is not how a man would go to work."

"We are well acquainted with how gentlemen do things," Faith said with a scowl, no doubt recalling her all too recent encounter with a deranged Sir Julian Wright, who had arranged a wager to publicly ruin Faith. The wager had become so out of hand that Lord Westwood had been kidnapped and Sir Julian had been killed.

"I agree with you," Hope said, but did not think this person deranged, merely selfish and calculating. But how far would they go to have their way?

"Hope, I want to call in my friends, at least for tonight. There will be too many people present for us to watch you alone, unless you do not dance and remain next to one of us the whole evening."

"And that would never do," Faith said quickly. "The best thing is for you to dance every dance and be happy."

"You know that will be difficult," Hope replied.

"But you see why it is necessary, do you not?" Westwood asked. "Rotham, Carew, Cunningham, Stuart, Fielding, Lord Gus—even Brosner are all willing to protect you. That would be eight sets if you include one with me."

Hope debated sharing her suspicions and decided it might be best. "I think I need to stay away from Rotham. I have a strong suspicion these threats are tied to his partiality for me."

Westwood frowned, and Hope could see he was considering the truth of the matter. "Be that as it may, would it not draw more atten-tion were you to ignore him?"

"Supposing all my dances were already spoken for? Is it too late to arrange that?" she asked. It would be much more difficult if she had to deny Rotham in person.

Westwood hesitated, but shook his head. "I will see it done."

"Thank you," she said softly. The last thing she wanted to do was offend Rotham, but she could not but think it was for the best.

As Jenkins placed the final touches on Hope's coiffure, there was another knock on the door. Westwood opened it and accepted a bouquet of flowers.

They were beautiful, bright yellow blooms, and Hope suspected they were from Rotham. Where else would flowers be found but from the estate?

Westwood handed the arrangement to her, then excused himself to make the arrangements with his friends as her other sisters, ready to go downstairs, came into the room to show off their gowns.

Patience wore rose, Grace a pale green. Joy had decided not to attend the ball and instead join the other young ladies who were not yet out.

"What lovely flowers!" Grace exclaimed as she spun about into the room, pretending to dance with the floral arrangement. "Are they pansies? Do they grow this time of year?"

"Anything can be grown in a greenhouse at an estate such as this, but they look more wild to me," Patience reflected on them as Grace set them on a side table. "I believe they may be pansies."

"Either way, they are quite pretty. Who are they from?" Grace asked.

"I have not yet had the chance to look," Hope stated the obvious as she pulled on her gloves to finish her toilette.

"Well, there is a note," Patience prodded.

Hope snatched the attached card, then her body froze as she read the words.

You cannot hide from me. Keep your distance or beware the shadows.

. . .

"Hope? What is it? You just turned as white as a ghost," Faith said.

Patience took it from her hands and read it aloud. "Keep your distance from whom?"

"Why is someone doing this to you? As disturbing as Sir Julian was, at least I knew who was threatening me," Faith declared. "I am glad Westwood is arranging for his friends to protect you."

"Maybe it would be safer if I stayed with Joy," Hope whispered, trying not to tremble.

"But Hope, if you do not come to the ball, then they win," Patience argued.

"I care not about winning. 'Tis not a duel! I just wish to be safe!"

"Whoever it is will be pleased if you hide," Patience insisted.

"Maybe it would be for the best if we leave on the morrow," Faith said.

"Do you not wish to know who is doing this?" Grace asked shrewdly.

"I just want it to stop," Hope pleaded as a tear rolled down her cheek.

"There is no guarantee it will stop, even if we leave," Patience reasoned.

Hope knew why Patience did not want to leave, and she had no desire to spoil her chances either.

"I can endure it for a little while longer," she said. "I would like to put an end to this once and for all." She stood up and took her fan from the table.

"You are quite certain?" Faith asked.

"Let us go before I change my mind."

IF THE SITUATION with Hope were not enough to occupy his mind, his parents were at loggerheads. Max had been walking through the hall earlier in the day when he'd heard them arguing and the Duke had finished by banishing the Duchess to the Dower House. What they had been arguing about, he could not say, but the Duke had been in a rage such as Max had not known he was capable of, and there was a little doubt that the Duchess had been the cause.

By the time Max intervened, the Duke was having a spell and had to take to his bed. Dr. Cafferty had diagnosed an apoplectic fit and had urged the Duke to rest and calm himself.

Neither the Duke nor Duchess was fit for company, so hopefully Diana could help him invent an excuse for neither of them attending the ball that evening. It was the worst possible time to have to leave his father in order to entertain over a hundred guests. Thankfully, his father's devoted valet was by his side.

The seating arrangements for dinner had quickly been altered, and Max presided over one end and Diana oversaw the other. With a sweet smile, she had announced that their father and mother were indisposed. As likely as not, everyone assumed it was due to the Duke's illness.

He had wanted to escort Hope into dinner again and shout to the world that she was his choice—his future duchess, but Hope had arrived late again and had not even looked at him. What the devil was going on?

Then he had to excuse himself early to stand in the receiving line with Diana, and thus not be able to exchange a single word or glance with his beloved since the day before. Had his passion scared her away? He could not think so. She had seemed willing to be kissed at the time—and had clung to him as much as he had to her.

He needed to speak with her—he intended to open the ball with her. There was not much time left, for guests continued to straggle in until the last minute. When he was finally free, he looked out over the crowd, but Brosner was already leading her onto the floor. "What the devil?" he muttered.

"What is wrong, Max?" Diana asked. "You are in quite a dudgeon."

"I am hiding my spleen well, then," he retorted. "I am quite livid, my dear. In fact, I should very much like to draw someone's cork!" he retorted.

She was looking out over the partners, taking their places in the first set. "Ah, I see Brosner beat you to her, did he? Well, you had better select someone else quickly before they are all standing waiting upon you to begin. I fully intend to become a *faux pas* by dancing with my husband." She waggled her eyebrows at him like they were young again and with a sly smile, sauntered away.

As he looked out over the sea of guests, laughter and banter filled the air. Gentlemen, dressed in their finely tailored coats, and ladies, arrayed in gowns of the most fashionable satins and silks, did not seem to realize the tension thrumming through him. He did not want to choose a new partner. He wanted to raise up an army to fight for his woman, as did Menelaus!

Perhaps, if he could find one of the Whitford sisters to dance with, he could discover what was happening. He first spotted Miss Patience, but she was already paired with Major Stuart. Grace was with Carew, which only left Lady Westwood. Perhaps he could convince Westwood to give up his wife. He headed in their direction.

He smiled as he approached. "Is there any way I could persuade you to let me open the ball with your wife, Westwood? I had been hoping to dance with Miss Whitford, but Brosner has beat me to her."

He saw the couple exchange glances and Westwood give a small nod.

"You will owe me a favour for this one, Rotham," Westwood said as he placed his wife's hand in Max's.

"Consider it done."

They took their places in the set. A country dance was not as ideal as some for conversing, but he would take what he could. "May I enquire how your sister is this evening?" he asked as they waited for the music to begin.

"To which one do you refer?" she asked with a twinkle in her eye.

She was going to be evasive. That was not good. "I am, of course, concerned about all of them, but in light of the circumstances, I was asking about Miss Hope in particular."

He saw her bite on her lower lip with indecision.

"Please tell me if something has happened."

The dance began, and he bowed. They circled one another, but yet she did not answer. Max was growing more impatient by the moment.

As they approached each other again, he pleaded with his eyes. If something else had happened, he needed to do something about it.

"I do not know if she would wish for me to tell you, but she has received another note, and she is even more convinced she must stay apart from you."

"What did it say to make her think that?"

"Keep your distance," she said hurriedly as they were forced to release each other and take a turn with their next partner.

It took Max a moment to consider the words. At first, he mistook her meaning; that she was telling *him* to keep his distance in the dance, but then it struck him. Was that what this was all about? Hope was being tormented because of him? He wasn't certain, because he also could have been hit with that lead ball…but if someone was warning Hope away from him, how much farther would they go?

"Therefore we have arranged for her to dance with other gentlemen tonight. I do hope you understand and will respect her wishes," she continued when they came together again, whilst Max's mind was still assimilating the possibilities.

"Of course, if she thinks that to be the best course, I will keep my distance from her tonight." She did only mean for that night, he hoped.

As the night progressed, watching Brosner, then Carew, then Cunningham, then Montford, then Stuart dance with Hope and not being able to have a turn himself was making him irritable in the extreme.

"It would help if you were not watching her like a fawning puppy," Westwood told him.

"Are you suggesting that I am ignoring my own partners?"

"I am not suggesting, I am telling you. They are only trying to help, so do not bite their heads off over it."

"You cannot tell me Brosner and Carew are uninterested."

"Her safety is what matters most at the moment."

"I agree, which is why I want to keep her close," Max argued.

Westwood shook his head. "If her suspicions are correct, then you being near to her is the biggest threat."

Max had to do something. "This latest letter your wife told me about…how did Hope receive it?"

"It was disguised within a bouquet of yellow flowers, possibly pansies, sent up by a footman. And before you ask, I have already questioned him. He said they were downstairs on a table in a large vase, waiting to be delivered. No one knows who they came from."

Max cursed. "Did you ask the gardener? It is most likely they came from the estate."

"Not yet," Westwood admitted. "There has not yet been time."

Max felt there was no time to waste, but it would be difficult for him to slip away from the ball. However, this was urgent and he would do it.

Westwood must have read his face. "Are you going now?" he asked. "Would it not be better if I went in your stead?"

"I think he will tell me more, though I appreciate the offer. Will you stand watchman on my behalf while I leave?"

Giving him a look of exasperation, Westwood nodded.

Max found his sister and broke the news to her.

"What am I supposed to tell people?"

"Whatever comes to mind. Tell them I am attending Father if needs be."

She shook her head and waved him on his way.

He left through the open terrace doors, praying the likes of Lady Matilda did not follow. Hopefully, Westwood would intercede if that was the case.

Once free of the house, he moved quickly through the gardens, just short of actually running. It was a cool, breezy evening after the previous day's storm, the smell of damp earth still redolent in the air. He entered the trees and followed the narrow footpath, thankful there was enough moon to light the way.

The Dower House was on the way to the gardener's cottage, and he saw the candles were lit, indicating his mother's inhabitance. Truthfully, he was grateful for her absence at the ball. The constant disdain and disapproval were wearying and tiresome.

As the gardener's thatched cottage and the greenhouses came into view, so did a large herbal garden. He walked up the path and knocked on the door, almost sure the gardener would have nothing helpful to say.

"How are you, MacKay?" Max asked.

"Me lord?" old man MacKay asked. He still bore the bushy beard that Max remembered, which had now greyed. His weathered face looked up at Max and wrinkled into a smile. "Is summat amiss?"

"I apologize for disturbing you in the evening, but it is important to ask. Did someone ask you for a bouquet of pansies today?"

"Nay, me lord. 'Twould be a strange thing for a bouquet this time 'o year."

"Could it have been something similar?"

The man's weathered face wrinkled and he shook his head. "'Te only flower that might resemble it be henbane, but 'twould be odd indeed, it bein' known to stupefy."

"Stupefy?" Max asked with surprise.

"It causes madness, me lord."

"Are they all over the estate?"

He shook his head. "Nay, me lord. We must keep it from the herds. 'Tis too poisonous to touch. But there be some in the herbal garden. Sometimes 'tis used as medicine."

"I see. Thank you for humouring me. Good evening to you."

"And to you, me lord."

Max walked back to the ball, considering what MacKay had said. Why henbane? And who would know where to find it? It did not yet appear that anyone had been harmed by the poisonous plant, but Max did not wish to take any chances.

As soon as he reached the house, he would immediately order a footman to remove the henbane from Hope's room.

CHAPTER 16

Despite her resolve to stay away from Rotham during the ball, Hope was conscious of him at every moment.

"You look lovely tonight," Lord Brosner said, drawing her attention back to him as they went through the motions of the dance.

"Thank you, my lord."

Rotham was dancing with Faith, and oh, how Hope would have loved to be in her sister's place! They seemed to be having a serious discussion, and she wanted to know every word.

"I have been wanting to speak with you, but you have been deuced difficult to find alone these days," he lamented.

"I apologize, my lord."

He smiled at her indulgently. "This is not the ideal place to ask, but I find I cannot wait any longer. Would it come amiss if I were to speak to your guardian?"

The words were so unexpected, that Hope almost lost her footing in the dance.

"Of course, I know you would like to be courted and wooed, but I did not wish to leave you with any doubt as to my intentions."

Hope knew she should be delighted by the declaration, yet inside she wanted to deny him. What could she say? She could not sever the connection.

"You do not need to answer me now. I can tell that I have astonished you."

"I am very flattered, my lord. I would not be averse to getting to know you better." That was the highest form of prevarication, but it was honest.

He smiled down at her, and he was handsome. He was just not Rotham. She desperately wanted to ask what his family would think, and if he was no longer in need of an heiress.

The next dance was with Lord Carew, and he was as charming as ever.

"How blows the wind these days, my dear? Are you in need of rescue?" His blue eyes twinkled.

"I always seem to be in need of it," she said, answering truthfully. She could not take Carew seriously and therefore felt at ease speaking her mind to him.

Unconsciously, her eyes searched the room for Rotham, who was now dancing with Vivienne Cunningham.

"Just say the words, my dear," Carew murmured in that half-teasing, half-serious way he had, which left you wondering what he really meant.

"I thank you, my lord. One of these days you will be punished for your chivalry when someone takes you up on your offer."

He laughed with his roguish smile. "It would serve Rotham right if you did."

"It would indeed," she agreed.

He laughed, then they spoke no more about it.

The next partner arranged for her was Freddy Cunningham. He was cheerfully oblivious to her inner turmoil—either that, or he was determined to make her forget about it.

Rotham was not dancing the set, she noticed, but was speaking with Lord Westwood all the while Mr. Cunningham was regaling her with tales about each of his new puppies. How she wished her only care in the world was the personality of an animal!

Lord Montford whirled by with Mr. Cunningham's sister in his arms, causing him to frown.

Hope looked at the couple for a quick moment and could see they were enchanted. An interesting development. Hope had not considered that Miss Cunningham might want someone else. She had assumed the young girl would accede to her parents' and the Duchess's wishes.

Hope's attention returned to Westwood and Rotham. Rotham was pointing outside, and Westwood seemed to be hesitant about whatever his friend was saying. Rotham then left through the open door.

"Where is he going?"

"Who?" Freddy asked, still watching his sister.

"Rotham has just left the ballroom through the open doors to the garden," she said a bit impatiently. "He looked in a bit of a hurry." Was she the only one who noticed his every partner, every drink, every move?

Freddy frowned. "Deuced odd time to leave his own ball. Must be meeting someone."

"An assignation?" She had never considered such a thing.

"I would not think so. He ain't taken with anyone but you," he answered frankly, not seeming to realize the awkwardness of the remark.

"What lies in that direction?" she asked.

He had to concentrate, she could tell, to both mind his steps and think about the layout of the estate. "Nothing besides the Dower House and the tenant cottages. Can't see why the devil he'd be going there during a ball."

Hope couldn't either.

The mystery was not resolved while she danced with Mr. Cunningham, and she longed to go after Rotham to see what he was about. However, with so many people watching over her, she knew she would not be able to slip out unobserved.

If only she could speak with Westwood!

The next set was a waltz, and she wondered what the chances were that Faith would trade her dance with Westwood. The rules of

London did not seem to apply at this house party with regards to dancing with one's husband.

Hope hurried across the ballroom to try to speak with them, but they were already taking the floor.

She saw Captain Fielding approach, and she wondered if he would be offended if she asked to sit the dance out. Small talk would be beyond her at the moment.

He bowed in front of her, a handsome man in Regimentals with medium chestnut hair and long, matching whiskers. "I have come to claim the next set with you, Miss Whitford."

She smiled. "I am feeling a little fatigued, sir. Would you mind terribly if we sit this one out? If there is another young lady you would like to dance with, I will sit with the Dowager." She indicated the far wall, where several of the matrons were sitting and chatting with animation.

He seemed to hesitate as though he would be defying a direct order.

"I assure you, I will stay by her side."

"Very well, Miss Whitford. There is a young lady with whom I should like to waltz," he said amiably.

Hope should not be so relieved, but this entire situation was unsettling in the extreme. On her way to the Dowager's side, she saw a movement just outside the door through which Rotham had left.

She looked about, and no one was watching her, so she merely stepped over the threshold, not desirous of jaunting about in the dark after the previous day's adventure. The cool breeze was welcome as her eyes tried to adjust to the darkness. However, there was nothing there. It must have been her imagination. Certainly, Rotham was nowhere to be seen. She looked up and watched the stars for a few minutes of the waltz, feeling safe enough just at the edge of the ballroom. As she turned to go in, a shrill voice stopped her.

"Are you looking for my son?"

"Your Grace. I needed some fresh air. I thought you were indisposed."

"I, too, needed some fresh air."

Was this an effort to be civil? Hope only wanted the conversation to end.

"Since our time is limited, I will get to the point. How much do you want?"

"I beg your pardon?"

"Come, now. Do not play the fool with me! A girl of your family and station must want something. I cannot fault that you have ambition, only that it is my son you have your sights set upon."

"This is distasteful in the extreme!" Hope protested as she realized what the Duchess had offered.

"I am glad you see it that way," she said, deliberately misunderstanding Hope.

"I cannot but be offended, madam," she said resolutely.

"Five thousand pounds," the Duchess offered provokingly.

"You may stop there, your Grace. No amount you offer would be amenable to me. You may not have a conscience or a soul, but I do, and accepting a sop such as you offer is repugnant to my very being!"

"You pretend to take the moral high ground with me? Everyone can be bought! Ten thousand pounds, and that is my final offer. Then you will leave this estate, never to return!" She growled the words, visibly shaking with anger.

"I will leave when my host asks me to, madam."

"I will see you and your sisters ruined," she threatened, with the look of the devil in her eyes—and Hope believed her.

Regardless of the threat, Hope refused to back down from this bullying. "You will do what you will regardless of what I say. I am returning to the Dowager."

"You will regret defying me!"

Hope turned on her heel and marched back into the ballroom, her face flushed and her pulse racing with fury.

MAX WALKED BACK towards the house, lost in thought. Whoever was doing this to Hope needed to be caught and held accountable. Unless

—and until—that happened, Hope was out of his reach, and that thought was unbearable. There had to be some clue, some connection that he was missing.

Much though he loathed the idea, he was afraid they were going to have to set a trap. Placing footmen as guards had only caused the person to be more creative with sending their vile notes.

But what kind of trap could they set that wouldn't be too risky for Hope? He could think of nothing. Moving chambers had not helped. He would have to consult with his friends to see what they thought.

A noise caused him to stop and listen. It was probably an animal, but he stepped off the gravelled path to see. The sound of hurried, agitated footsteps fell to his ears. A disgruntled servant?

Angered mutterings could be heard as they grew closer, but he could barely discern that it was a female voice, not what they said. Shrinking back further into the shadows, he waited for the person to come into sight. "What the devil?" he whispered, then stepped out into the path.

Startled, her Grace grabbed at her chest. "Rotham! Whatever are you doing out here?"

"I ask the same of you, your Grace." He spoke her title as an insult.

"As you well know, your father has banished me to the Dower House. Am I a prisoner that I may not walk outside?" she asked in an offended tone.

"Is that all you have been doing?" Max could not but ask. She was dressed for the ball, and Max wondered if she'd been to the house.

"I did not go into the ball if that is what you are asking, though it is still my house!" she said indignantly.

"But you were watching," he said, with sickening realization.

"Why should I not? Lord Montford is making up to Vivienne Cunningham. You need to redirect your attention back to where it belongs, Rotham!"

"Good for Monty. He will make Miss Cunningham an excellent husband."

She huffed her disapproval. "You enjoy thwarting me, do you not, ungrateful son? Well, I will have you know that Miss Whitford has agreed to take a sum in exchange for staying away from you," she imparted with pleasure.

Max narrowed his gaze. "I do not believe you."

"No? Did she dance with you this evening?"

Max opened his mouth to argue, then closed it again.

"You made her an offer, did you not? Did she accept it?"

Good God, is that what had happened? How could she know Max had declared himself to Hope? "You promised not to meddle."

"I did what I thought was necessary for the dukedom. You may not hold your name and blood in high esteem, but I have not forgotten what is due our family and country! I have sacrificed everything—everything!—for this family. You will not destroy everything I stand for with one callous act. You may keep her on the side if you cannot control your base urges, but your children will not be of inferior blood."

Max seethed, his rage barely contained, on the brink of unleashing. "I can, and I will, marry whom I choose. You have nothing to say to it. You have not earned that right. Do not preach to me of what is due our name. The only role you played in bringing up a duke was giving birth to me."

The Duchess was shaking with fury. "How dare you?"

"If anything, your opposition is all the more reason to go forward with the marriage."

"You ungrateful, arrogant wretch!" she seethed.

"You, madam, will interfere no more, or you will see yourself removed far from Davenmere and anything to do with it. Do I make myself clear?"

She did not answer, she only glared. "You will regret this day."

"I already do, your Grace. I already do. And if you harm one hair on Miss Whitford's head, you will be paid in kind tenfold."

"We will see about that!" She turned and stormed off to the Dower House, leaving Max standing there wondering what had just happened. He stood still for a few minutes, trying to bring his boiling blood back to some semblance of calm. Never before had anyone caused him to lose control in such a manner. He was known for his cold control at all times.

Had she been the one tormenting Hope? Max feared it was so as realization struck him with the force of a knife to the chest. The extent of her obsession had made her hysterical, and she felt it was her duty to keep Max away from Hope.

The handwriting had not been hers, but her maid or her secretary would have obeyed her commands without daring to demur.

It was also very plausible that she could have locked Hope in the bath house and then unlocked it again. How else would she have known he had declared himself, had she not been watching and listening?

The more he considered, the more sick he felt. She was also known to be an excellent shot. But had she aimed to kill or merely to frighten?

There was also the easy access to the henbane: she was one of the few who would have known where it was.

In his life, he had known his mother to be many things, but he would never have supposed her capable of this. It was not so much hatred for Hope as it was pride of the cursed dukedom. Hope had dared to get in the way of her Grace's plans.

Max had not accused the Duchess outright because he did not wish her to know his suspicions in the small chance that it was not her. It would only make the situation worse. However, he would set men to watch the Duchess at all times, because he feared she had lost any vestige of sanity. She had looked prepared to commit murder just then. But had she tried to *kill* Hope? By God, if he discovered it was her intention, it would be nigh impossible not to commit matricide.

There was not enough proof, but he needed to stop the persecution before it went any further, and before anyone discovered who was doing this. The Duchess might not think he valued their lineage, but if her actions were discovered, it would forever be attached to the Davenmere name.

How could he catch the Duchess in the act, while at the same time preventing any harm to come to Hope?

He could not think of any solution where he would not have to confide in her. Knowing Hope, she would not welcome him back unless she knew she was no longer in danger. She would not be satisfied unless she knew who had been doing this.

The possibility of this ending well was slim.

With a heavy heart, he returned to the ball, wishing it were over. He was not certain he could paste on the false façade and pretend everything was as it should be when it was anything but.

He stood at the terrace doors from which he had exited earlier. He watched and pondered how to handle his mother and Hope. Falling in love should have been the happiest time of his life, yet it seemed Hope was correct in that she needed to stay away from him. As he watched her dancing with Major Stuart, he knew he would not rest until she was his.

CHAPTER 17

*H*ope had been exhausted enough from dancing that she was able to sleep without tossing and turning or having nightmares, which was quite surprising after the quarrel with the Duchess.

When she woke the next morning, Faith had already gone, and a maid was bringing her hot water. Hope got down from the bed and pulled on her wrapper as she tucked her feet into her slippers. Out of habit, she splashed her face and patted it dry, then unravelled her plaits, and began to brush her hair.

"Have you need of anything else, miss? Many guests are leaving today, so there is a great bustle downstairs," the maid told her.

"I would like a cup of tea."

"Yes, miss," she said, bobbing a curtsy. "Lady Westwood told me to say she's in her room if you have need of anything, and just to knock."

Hope went to the balcony and opened the doors to inhale the fresh air. The sound of the river was so soothing to her spirit that she could almost forget all the horrible things that had happened. Desperately, she wanted to think they weren't real, but the Duchess's words had erased any doubt that she was the likely source of the threats. The only person who had expressed outright disapproval of her was the

Duchess. Why would a duchess be threatened by such a one as her? The only possible reason was if she seriously considered Hope a contender for Rotham's hand...it wasn't enough that Hope had already decided she could not have him.

Which meant that she could never be with Rotham. It would be best for her to leave—especially with the Duke having taken a turn for the worse. She suspected many of the guests would also be leaving, which at least would not make her own departure—and the reason for it—so obvious.

The maid returned with the tea, and having prepared a cup, Hope sat and tried to find comfort in the beauty that surrounded her.

Leaving Davenmere would be difficult, because it also meant severing herself from Rotham forever. If there were any other way... she shook her head. It was no use. How could she tell him her suspicions? How could she tell him that she suspected his mother of trying to bribe her and possibly kill her? Hope could not do that, nor could she live with being the cause of such a rift.

It did not appear they were close or even affectionate, that was true enough, but there was nothing more sacred to the aristocracy than their good name. Yet, after his tender love and kisses at the bath house, living without Rotham was too much to contemplate. She choked on a sob and let some tears fall until she was resigned to her fate.

A knock on the door disturbed her hard-won composure, and she wiped at her eyes and checked herself in the mirror before opening the door.

"Rotham! What are you doing here?" She was hardly dressed to receive visitors!

"I have Westwood's permission to speak with you. May I come in?"

She looked both ways down the hall, then stepped back to admit him.

"Forgive the presumption, but I needed to speak with you."

The look on his face was more akin to pain than amour, and instantly Hope feared the Duke had died. "Is it your father?"

"No." He shook his head. "He is stable for now."

"Thank goodness," she said with genuine relief.

"May we sit down?" He indicated the chairs flanking the fireplace, and she took one. He sat opposite and then seemed reluctant to speak.

"What is it you wish to speak of?" It was so very unlike him to hesitate.

"My mother," he began before closing his mouth. "Forgive me, this is difficult to say."

"Take your time," she said as she longed to reach out and comfort him. But that would only make the parting worse, so she clasped her hands together in her lap.

He swallowed hard before speaking again. "I believe my mother may be responsible for the notes and the mishaps you have suffered."

Hope was shocked that he had realized it.

"You are not surprised, are you?" he asked, noticing her lack of reaction.

"I fear it is so," she said carefully.

"Why did you not come to me?"

"How does one say, 'I believe your mother dislikes me so much that she might have tried to kill me?'"

He closed his eyes as though in pain.

"She confronted me last night at the ball. She tried to pay me to leave and never have anything to do with you again. It was the vitriol I saw in her eyes that convinced me. Then I started to consider each incident and knew it had to be someone with intimate knowledge of the estate and grounds. No one else has the motivation to see me disposed of."

"Did she succeed?"

"In purchasing my acquiescence? How can you ask such a thing?"

"Because, my love, I can see why anyone would be hesitant to align themselves with madness!"

"You fear insanity?" She shook her head. "This is passion, delusion. I would have nothing to say to that..." She could not finish what she wished to say aloud. "However, she will never change her mind, and I will not be the cause of division in your family."

"You are not the cause, Hope. The Duchess has already severed the connection. The Duke has banished her. The mistake he made was not putting her under guard. I have already rectified the matter and after the Duke's death, she will no longer be at Davenmere."

Hope bit her lower lip and closed her eyes. To think that she had been the cause of such a thing. How was she to live with it?

"Please talk to me, Hope," Rotham pleaded.

"What is there to say? I never wanted this to happen."

"None of this is your fault. Every action and every thought are entirely her own, as are the consequences."

"If you married as your family wished, would this not be avoided?"

"How can you ask that of me? Would you rather see me enter into a loveless marriage? My mother has never cared for me as a person, only as a title. I will never give my allegiance to that. I will honour my duty to the country and the people I am responsible for, but to ask me to enter it into a white marriage when I love *you*, is something I find impossible."

Hope's throat was choking with tears, and she could not stop her chin from trembling. Before she knew what was happening, Rotham had pulled her into his arms and was holding her.

"Sweet Hope, say you will be mine."

It was what she wanted more than anything. Before she could answer, he was showering her with kisses.

"But supposing the one responsible is not her?" she asked.

He sighed longingly as though he would rather do anything than discuss the situation. "That is what I came to speak to you about. We have no proof, but regardless of the outcome, she will not remain here. We could wait a little longer to see if the threats stop now that the Duchess is under guard. We could also set a trap, but that would leave you too vulnerable."

"I am willing to do whatever is necessary to erase any doubt. What do you think we should do?"

"If we announce our betrothal and wed quickly, for the sake of the Duke, there is nothing anyone could do. Surely that would silence whoever objects to the marriage once the knot is properly tied."

"You truly mean it?" She searched his eyes as if to find the answer beyond his words.

"Have I not been saying so?"

"It was only a week ago you were uncertain and considering several other ladies. It is an irreversible step and I would not want you to regret your choice."

"Dearest Hope, witnessing the other ladies in the same situation as you has only reaffirmed my conviction that you are the only choice for me."

Hope wanted more than anything to believe it. "You are certain you wish to marry in such haste?"

"I have no doubts in my mind whatsoever," he said earnestly. "May we tell everyone today? I know it would please my father enormously."

"If you think it is for the best to do so now, then, by all means. Have you spoken to Westwood?"

Rotham chuckled. "I have. He has been waiting impatiently for us to come to an agreement."

Hope smiled, and before she could reply, Rotham grasped her face in both hands.

"I am also impatient for you to be mine." His lips descended to hers and he kissed her with an urgency and tenderness that left no doubt as to his feelings.

She was still stunned when he broke away.

"I will return for you in an hour and we will first go and tell the good news to the Duke." He kissed her one more time before casting her a look of such longing that it warmed her straight to her toes. "One hour," he said firmly, and on the words, promptly left.

MAX FELT like dancing as he left Hope's room. In just a short time, she would be his, and the intolerable state of affairs with the Duchess would be over when she left Davenmere. He refused to let her overshadow their happiness.

"I trust your meeting went well?" Westwood asked, one eyebrow raised as he stepped out of his chamber.

Max grinned like a small child. "Indeed, it did. We will tell everyone today. I am coming back in an hour to escort her downstairs to tell the news to the Duke."

Westwood shook his hand and gave him a hug. "Welcome to the family, officially."

"What is this?" Lady Westwood appeared in their doorway.

"I should let your sister tell you the news."

"Has she accepted you?" She squealed with delight and clapped her hands.

"We think it best to announce the betrothal today and wed soon—for the sake of the Duke, of course."

"Of course," she agreed knowingly and boldly embraced him.

"Would you and the Dowager be able to make the arrangements with Diana? The Duchess will not be available." That was a kind way of saying she was unwelcome.

"I would be delighted," she said. "Send her to me once you have told her the news yourself. I will go to Hope in just a moment."

Max excused himself to do just that. Diana gave much the same reaction as Lady Westwood had done.

"Oh, Max! I have longed for you to find someone who will make you happy."

"As have I." He then explained that their own mother was under guard at the Dower House and why.

Diana was shocked. "I knew she was overly besotted with Davenmere and her pride in the family's lineage, but not once did it occur to me she would attempt to harm Hope."

"She will no longer stand in my way."

"I am delighted for you. Is it a secret?"

Max shook his head. "We intend to marry quickly because of Father's condition."

He did not care if everyone knew before the formal announcement. He wanted to shout it from the rooftops.

"Shall I make your excuses to the guests who are departing?" It was a rhetorical question.

"You are the best of sisters, Diana," he said with a quick buss on her cheek.

Next, he went to the Duke's chambers to make certain he would be able to receive them. He was resting peacefully in his bed, so Max decided to wait until Hope was with him. But as he turned to leave, his father called out to him.

"Max? Did you need me for something?"

"I was only seeing how you are faring. I was going to bring Miss Whitford to visit you in a little while, if you are up to visitors."

"Stay for a moment. It is a dead bore lying in bed all the time."

Max chuckled. "Shall I send for your dogs to keep you company?"

His father smiled crookedly. "Would you? I think that would be just the thing."

Max looked at the valet, who was standing nearby, and inclined his head. This conversation was better conducted in private.

"Nelson and Hector have been kept apart only so not as to disturb his Grace."

"I am well enough now, Hartley."

Reluctantly, and making sure Max understood that dogs were beneath the dignity of a duke's man, the valet left to send for the pets. Max was certain much of his ire was for missing the details of the conversation.

"Does this mean you've finally asked Miss Whitford to be your duchess?"

"I have asked her to be my wife. I am still hoping you will outlive me," Max said earnestly.

"Foolish boy," he said fondly. "I've no desire to do that."

"I was going to bring her here to tell you the news, so act duly surprised, if you will."

"Of course," the Duke agreed. He paused, and then grew solemn. "Have you heard news of the Duchess? I assume you know what happened?"

"I heard you having a great row and that she was sent to the Dower House."

"Yes." The Duke sighed heavily. "I am afraid your mother has become unhinged. She was talking some wild nonsense about wanting me to denounce Miss Whitford. I was afraid she would do the chit harm."

"She very nearly succeeded. Unfortunately, I found her wandering the grounds during the ball and I have now set footmen to guarding her."

"Stupid woman! To think she alone knows best who would suit you. What is worse, she considers herself above the redemption of any authority!"

Max did not want to upset his father, but he felt he should inform him of his intentions, in case the Duke lived longer than expected. "Your Grace, I intend to send her away from here."

He heaved another heavy sigh of disappointment. "I daresay that would be for the best. You will need to think of a plausible story."

"I thought to put it out that she was removing to the Continent for warmer climes."

He nodded with resignation. "Perhaps, my boy, when I have gone?"

Max hated to discuss such things, but knew it would ease his father's mind. "As you wish."

"I suppose I should dress now, if you are bringing your bride to me. I cannot be greeting her like this," he said with a smile.

"Of course. I am going to the vault to find the ring."

When Hartley returned with a couple of the Duke's older dogs, which greeted their master with unleashed joy, the conversation was over.

Max watched for a moment with fondness, then left to retrieve the Davenmere ring before returning to fetch Hope.

He entered the Duke's study, where the estate's offices adjoined the muniment room, in which the vaults containing the Davenmere jewels were located.

Abernathy was delighted when Max told him of his errand, and was only too happy to oblige him by producing the large oval ruby, encased in a circlet of triangle-shaped diamonds.

"May I say, my lord, that we are very pleased by this news," the steward remarked as though he represented the whole estate.

"As am I, Abernathy," he said, taking the ring from the steward's hands.

Rarely had Max given the jewel any thought—only he'd known it would one day be given to his bride.

"If you will also be so good as to have the Davenmere parure cleaned and made ready for the wedding, I would be obliged. It will take place very soon."

"I have already taken the liberty of doing so, my lord. It is ready whenever your lordship desires."

"Excellent."

Max was still smiling as he left the offices and began to return to Hope. On the way, he saw his brother.

"Gus, old boy! I have hardly seen you since the first day you arrived."

His brother looked mischievous. "I have not been hiding from you, Max."

"No, I do not suppose you have. I have been somewhat preoccupied."

"Yes, and the Duchess is in a pucker about it," he said as though this was nothing new, which it wasn't.

"She has filled your ears with her vitriol, I take it?"

"Her Grace is feeling very ill used, indeed. Better your problem than mine, Max."

Max shook his head. "The Duchess will soon be far away from here. Her health prefers a warmer climate."

"Is that how the wind blows? Serving her her just deserts, are you?" Gus asked with amusement.

"I wish it were not the case, but yes."

Max heard a clock chime the hour and realized he was late. He clapped a hand on his brother's back. "I must go. Wish me happy!"

Max heard Gus' laughter from behind him.

Now a few minutes late, Max rushed to the east wing, near to bursting with excitement. The footmen were not at their posts and Max frowned. Had something happened?

He broke into a run towards Hope's room and knocked. When there was no answer, he was close to being in a panic and threw open the door. "Hope?"

CHAPTER 18

*H*ope could not contain her excitement. When she had closed the door behind Rotham, she let out of squeal of delight. Knowing she did not have much time to prepare, she rang for Jenkins. She wanted to look her best for the meeting with the Duke.

It was still hard to fathom that Rotham had chosen her despite the Duchess' objections. But how could she deny his pleas for happiness? She was his choice, and if he was willing to make that step, she would trust him.

Jenkins entered, and saw the smile on Hope's face. "Oh, miss! Never tell me he has proposed!"

Hope nodded. "We are to seek the Duke's blessing in one hour. We must hurry!"

Jenkins moved with purpose, and was soon curling Hope's hair.

There came another knock on the door, and her sister, Faith, entered. She held out her arms and came over to give Hope a tearful hug.

"I pray those are tears of happiness?" Hope asked.

"Of course they are! I wish you all to find what I have."

Hope smiled. She wanted that as well. Faith stayed for a few minutes while Jenkins helped her to finish dressing.

"You need not wait. Rotham is coming to escort me himself."

"Very well. Will you find me afterwards? I want to hear everything!"

"I will seek you out as soon as I may, Faith," Hope assured her.

Jenkins finished dressing her hair and helped her into her gown. "What do you think of jewellery? I am inclined to think it would be best to wear pearls. He will be giving you a ring, I imagine."

"I trust your judgement," Hope said, trying to contain her excitement.

The maid left with ten minutes to spare. Hope danced around the room, unable to believe the turn in fortune when she'd been in complete despair the day before.

There was another knock on the door and Hope rushed over to open it. "You are early!" she said, then stopped as she realized it was only one of the footmen placed there to guard her.

He bowed. "Lord Rotham has sent me to escort you to the Duke."

Hope was a little disappointed, but she was sure Rotham had his reasons. Anyway, she would see him in a few minutes.

She followed the footman into the hall and down a series of corridors along which she had not been before. It was incredible to think she would soon be mistress of all of this! In time, she would learn her way, but for today, she did not pay attention. She was too pleased with the world.

They came to a wing where there were three large carved doors, the one on the left bearing the Duke's coat of arms, the one in the centre with the Davenmere crest, and the one on the right with that of the Duchess.

"I have been asked to show you to her Grace's apartments, which will one day be yours. His lordship will receive you there."

Hope thought perhaps it was a little odd, given that his mother had been recently sent away from there, and the Duke not yet dead, but if that was what Rotham wished, then she would not argue.

The footman opened the door for her and she walked inside before he entered behind her and locked the door. That was when she knew something was very, very wrong. She did not even have the ability to take note of her surroundings, other than that it appeared she was in some type of antechamber and that dogs were barking somewhere within the house.

"Forgive me, miss," she heard before a cloth was put over her nose and mouth and pulled tightly behind her head.

She struggled against her capture. "Don't fight, miss. It will only go worse for you. I have no wish to hurt you."

"Then let me go," she mumbled against the tight binding across her mouth. Thankfully, he had not thrust anything into her mouth.

He pulled her towards the wall and opened a cupboard. "I have to put something over you now, miss."

He threw a burlap bag over the top of her, then pushed her inside the cupboard, which wobbled beneath her, making her shake with terror. Was she in a service lift?

He spoke down through a tunnel. "Clear," a reply echoed back to them, and she felt a rope pull, then the conveyance began to move downward. It felt as though she was sinking beneath the Earth, when she came to a sudden stop.

Another set of hands picked her up and lifted her from the box and placed her in what felt to be a cart. *Good God, they were carting her off like a sack of laundry!*

She began to squeal before the second voice scolded her. "There's no one about here, miss. You might as well save your breath."

There were no sounds other than the roll of the wheels beneath the cart, and she feared he was right. Shifting her attention to her surroundings, she did not think they were within the house any longer, although perhaps they could be in the cellars, or even a dungeon. Certainly Davenmere was old enough and large enough to have such a thing. It was much cooler and smelt of damp earthiness, and she could well believe she was in a cave.

The cart stopped for a moment and a heavy door creaked open with a rush of air.

Where was he taking her? The farther away from the house she was, the longer it would take for someone to find her.

Surely Rotham must realize by now that she was missing. He

would not think she would leave for a walk at such a time as this, would he? How long would it be until anyone realized?

Hope heard the sound of running water, but was certain they had not returned upwards to the level of the ground. Was this some kind of cave beneath the surface?

She had heard of such things, but had never seen one. Would Rotham even think to look there?

Spray wet her sack as they seemed to pass beneath a fall of water. Her spirits sank further and further as she seemed to be hidden beyond being found.

A wave of sickness caused bile to rise in her throat, and she would have retched had she had anything to eat that day.

Knowing who the malefactor was only deepened the comprehension that she and Rotham might never be together. Hope had to escape from there!

The cart stopped again, followed by the sound of a key being forced into a lock and turned before the man struggled to heave open a door. She was gently raised from the cart and placed upon the damp, chilled earth, a sensation most unwelcome and stark in her wet gown.

"I will be back to visit you later. There's a lantern and a blanket and some water."

He touched her again, and she flinched. "I am only removing the sack from your head, miss."

Hope sat still and allowed him to do that. It was only a small relief when she looked around and saw her small prison. She pulled the gag from her mouth as he began to leave her.

"Please don't do this!" she begged.

She debated whether she could push past him and escape, but he was probably a foot taller than she and several stones heavier. Without knowing where she was, or which way to go, it would be nearly impossible to evade him.

"How long will she leave me here?" Hope asked, needing some small crumb to hang on to.

"That I cannot say, miss. I promise I will come and see how you go on if it is to be very long."

With that she had to be grateful, because he closed and locked the door. How long would the lantern last?

Rotham would inflict dire retribution on his mother for this, she knew. She only prayed she herself did not die of cold first. There was little doubt in Hope's mind that the Duchess would kill to have her way. Hope gave in to the fear and began to sob with wretchedness.

MAX WAS IN AGONY. He knew that the Duchess was responsible for Hope's disappearance, yet he still threw open every door and window and began yelling for Westwood.

He ran and knocked on the door of his friend's apartments, but there was no answer. They must have already gone downstairs. Furiously, he pulled on the bell-rope. He wanted the entire house turned upside down, and he did not care who knew what the Duchess had done.

When, at last, a maid came into the hall, he practically shouted, "Go and fetch Lord Augustus, Lord Westwood, and any other of the gentlemen you can find. Tell them it is urgent!"

The Dowager Lady Westwood stepped into the hall from her chamber. "Is something amiss, Rotham? Forgive me, but I could not help but overhear."

"Hope is missing. I was supposed to meet her here a few minutes ago to go to visit the Duke. I know she would not have left of her own accord."

Concern crossed her features. "I think the girls are still in their apartments. I will see if they know anything."

Gilford arrived in a hurry, looking distressed. "My lord?"

"Who were the footmen to be on duty at this hour?"

Gilford looked around and realized they were missing. "Why, John and Thomas, sir. I made sure they had arrived at their posts. Where could they have gone?"

"Moreover, where have they taken Miss Whitford? She is not in her chamber and was to wait for me here. Make enquiries as quickly as possible. Check all of the doors and send Mrs. Watson to me immediately."

"Yes, my lord," he said and hurried away in as much of a panic as Rotham had ever seen him. It was good that he understood.

The Whitford sisters rushed into the hall, and Lady Westwood was with them. "Is Hope not here?" She was pale and looked alarmed. "But she was waiting for you specifically."

"It is as I feared. Someone has either kidnapped her or lured her away under false pretences," Max all but shouted, nearly pulling his hair out in his anguish.

Westwood arrived with Gus, Carew, Montford, Cunningham, Stuart, and Fielding. They looked ready to hunt. Quickly, Max explained his fears without fully implicating the Duchess. There would be time enough later for that. Now, the most important thing was finding Hope before any harm came to her.

"I think we need to do this methodically. She cannot have been gone more than an hour, at the most," Westwood reasoned aloud.

"I would say, not even above half an hour," Lady Westwood added. "I went to her room and stayed with her while she dressed."

"At least that limits how far they might have gone."

"I do not think we should waste time searching the house, but for the sake of thoroughness, I would ask you ladies to take that task under the direction of Mrs. Watson." He turned to the Dowager. "My lady, if you would discreetly gather the rest of the party and help account for them while we conduct a search? I would ask Courtenay and Lady Diana to assist you."

Max began to pace about as he thought frantically. "Where do you think she could have been taken?"

"Perhaps it would save time to put the dogs on the scent?" Gus suggested.

"An excellent idea," Max agreed. "Two are in the Duke's chambers as we speak."

Lady Westwood entered Hope's rooms and returned with some items for the dogs to smell as Mrs. Watson arrived and led the ladies away to search within the house. Meanwhile, Max racked his brain for places the Duchess could have taken Hope. "Let us remove to the study where the maps are," he said and led the way as the others followed.

"I will fetch the dogs from Father and meet you there," Gus said.

"Tell the grooms to prepare to search as well," Max ordered as they parted.

When they reached the study, Gilford was there, waiting with two of the footmen.

"My lord, this is Jack and James. They have something to tell you."

The two young men, with barely eighteen years if Max had to guess, looked terrified.

"You may speak freely. Miss Whitford could be in danger. Do you understand?"

"Yes, my lord," they answered.

"Tell his lordship what you told me," Gilford ordered impatiently.

"Tommy and John offered to take our post this morning."

"Is that all? Did you see or hear anything untoward?"

"I saw Tommy leading Miss Whitford towards the ducal apartments," Jack said.

"You are certain of that?" Max asked.

"Ain't nothing else that way, my lord."

He was correct. Max nodded. "If that is all you can tell me, then you will be best employed assisting with the search."

"There is one more thing, my lord," James said. "It may not be related, but I seen the Duchess speaking with Tommy and passing him notes."

"You have done well in telling me, lad."

"Also, my lord, no one has left the house by any of the outer doors," Gilford added.

Gus returned with the excited dogs, while Westwood was already organizing the search. "Let us divide into pairs. Gus knows this estate best and can go with some of the grooms. Freddy, you and Carew take the western direction towards your estate, Monty and I can take the south lawn and then I will take the direction of the river with more grooms."

"Max," Gus said. "Father thinks he heard voices coming from the Duchess's chambers just a short time ago. He said the dogs were barking and would not be hushed."

"I looked inside, but the only thing amiss was the door to the service lift cupboard was wide open. Do you think she could have been removed from the house that way?"

Max cursed. "That did not even occur to me! But why through the Duchess's apartment? There is one near the guest chambers in the east wing."

"But the ones in the central wing are the only ones which go to the level of the cellars," Gus reminded him.

"The river!" Both Gus and Max exclaimed at the same time. "There is a tunnel through the cellars to the river."

Westwood held up a hand. "Has anyone yet been to question the Duchess?"

"No," Max confessed. "She will not have done the work herself."

"But you could very well save a great deal of time if you can convince her to tell us where Hope is," Westwood said with sound reasoning.

Max hesitated because he wanted to search for Hope, but he knew his friend was right. "Someone had better come with me, because I cannot be held responsible for my actions with her."

"I will do so. If Gus does not mind staying here to superintend the search. I think your inclination that she was taken through the cellars to the river is a good one, but where would she be conveyed to from there?"

"It feeds all the way into the Trent. And with the recent rains, the current will be fast," Freddy said.

"Head in that direction, all of you. Perhaps you may catch them. We will go to the Dower House."

Max and Westwood set off at a run, and Max prayed that he could control his fury enough to extract information from his mother quickly.

He burst through the doors of the Dower House, breathing heavily, and even the guard was taken aback. "Where is she?" he demanded.

"The drawing room, my lord."

Max took the stairs two at a time, Westwood right behind him.

She was sitting there, looking demure and composed, but he was not fooled. Ice flowed through her veins.

"Rotham. Westwood. To what do I owe the honour?"

"Please dispense with the small talk. I know you have kidnapped Miss Whitford and I want to know where she is."

She smiled with pleasure, but it was evil. "Yes, I admit I have had her removed, but I will never tell unless you renounce this ridiculous plan to wed her."

Within seconds, he pounced upon her, his hands encircling her neck, choking her with a ferocious grip.

He felt Westwood prying him backwards. "Killing her will solve nothing, and will certainly not help us find Hope more quickly."

Max knew Westwood was right, but he was desperate. Reluctantly, he relaxed his murderous grip on her neck. Red finger marks marred her white skin—and her eyes protruded like a toad's. At the thought, he wiped his hands on his breeches and took a hasty breath. The desire to snap her neck raged as fire in his veins.

Her maid ran to her side, casting a look of scorn at Max.

"You will rot in hell alongside her," he warned. "You will both leave Davenmere today, and never return, unless you tell me where you have taken her!"

"Your father will never stand for this," the Duchess said with haughty grandeur.

"He has already given his blessing. Unfortunately, the stay on your sentence until his death will be revoked after your actions today. Do you realize that ball also hit me?"

"You were not supposed to move. I only intended to frighten her."

"And all for what? Was it worth it? Miss Whitford will be my bride within days, regardless of this wicked deed."

She cackled. "If you can find her. She will be dead by morning, otherwise."

"Your Grace, I beg of you," Westwood said calmly. "Do you truly wish to murder a girl guilty of no other crime than attracting your son? Even being a Duchess will not save you from the noose."

"What does that matter when everything I stand for will be in ruins?" she asked self-righteously. "I am doing this for your own good, Rotham! One day you will thank me!"

Max and Westwood exchanged glances of desperation.

"I warned the scheming strumpet to stay away. She made her choice and is reaping her just deserts!"

"Where is she?" Max growled into her face.

"Somewhere cold, dark and wet, where she belongs." Her eyes narrowed as she clearly relished her words.

Max could see they would get no more help from her. "Pack as much as you can in the next two hours. You will leave before nightfall. If ever I see you again, I will not answer for my actions. And if Hope dies, you had better pray I never find you, because I will hunt you to the gates of hell."

"I consider it my duty to preserve the purity of the Davenmere line. If I must be a martyr, then so be it."

"Come," Westwood said, pulling his arm. "We will gain no more from this quarter."

"You will never find her in time!" she called after them with savage pleasure.

Max barked his instructions for the Duchess' banishment to the footman on duty at the door before running as fast as he might towards the river.

CHAPTER 19

The desperation was excruciating. If he had been in a panic before he spoke to the Duchess, then now he was in utter despair. His imagination was running riot into the hellish possibilities of where Hope could be on the vast estate and beyond. The clock was ticking, according to her Grace.

"Do you think she has had Hope thrown in the river?" he asked Westwood. Could Hope even swim? He should know this about her.

"It sounded more as though she was in a dungeon," Westwood said.

"We do not have a dungeon, but perhaps we should also search the cellars for any hidden places. It does not make sense to put her there, but if that is where she is imprisoned, then we should be able to find her."

"Perhaps she was deliberately trying to divert us on the wrong path?" Westwood asked.

"It is a possibility, but something tells me it is unlikely. She seemed confident in her capabilities to thwart us."

When they reached the river's edge, footmen, grooms on horseback, and whippers-in with hounds were searching every inch as far as Max could see. Those on horseback were combing the edges of the banks on both sides as the river flowed swiftly along. Max did not see his brother, but Freddy and Captain Fielding were leading the search outside.

"Have you found anything at all?" he asked. "The Duchess was very little help."

"They have not caught her scent up here. Gus took two of the dogs down to the cellars to try to pick it up there. Hopefully he is having better luck! We will continue to follow downstream."

Max blew out a breath of frustration, but tried to remain calm. "I will return to the house and find him, then."

As he approached the house, he saw Gilford waiting for him. "All the servants and guests have been questioned, my lord. No one has seen anything. We are still searching the attics and more obscure places within the house. His lordship and some of the other gentlemen are searching the cellars."

Max and Westwood hurried through the house, down through the kitchens and then down another narrow set of stairs to the cellars. Max was acutely aware of things he'd never before considered, like the drop in temperature and the dark dampness as they descended, but was it enough alone to kill Hope if she wasn't found quickly? He did not think so, but perhaps there was something he was missing. It did not quite fit the picture the Duchess had painted. They encountered servants moving sacks of flour and vegetables, kegs of beer and ale, and shelves of wine, looking behind these items into storage cupboards that were scarcely used.

"Where is Lord Augustus?" he asked the under butler, who was directing the search.

"The dogs picked up a scent through the tunnel and they went that way," the servant said as he pointed. A large oak door separated the house from the tunnel, and it was partially jammed open.

"The tunnels have been blocked off for years, but someone has recently moved the shelves which obstructed the doors," the man explained.

If that were the case, then the Duchess had been plotting this in some detail, which lent a more sinister turn to her actions than he had thought her capable of.

"I suggest you take a lantern, my lord." The man took one off the wall and handed it to Max.

With a grateful nod, he took the lamp and pulled open the heavy door. There were tracks in the earthen floor from some type of cart, and he could see where the dogs' and other footprints had been.

He prayed silently, as he and Westwood bent down and hurried along, that the dogs had found her.

"Where does this lead?" Westwood asked.

"A grotto or some type of underground folly, I believe. It was forbidden to us in my youth and I had forgotten about it. It was walled off when it fell into disrepair."

When they reached the end of the tunnel, there was another heavy steel door that led to the outside. It opened with a rush of air into a large cavernous space and a series of caves where part of the river overflowed through a wall to form a waterfall. Max didn't know whether they were natural or whether they had been carved into the side of the rocks when grottoes had been all the rage during the past century. He vaguely recalled them being closed off when he was a boy after a series of falling rocks had made it too dangerous for four children to explore.

He saw his brother with Carew, Stuart, and Montford, looking around while the dogs were circling the place. There were a few walkways around the edges of the pool.

"What has happened?" Max asked.

"They had her scent, but it stopped here. There is nothing but these large caves down here."

Elaborate carvings of Roman gods frolicking were etched into the walls, and water trickled, in a fall from the ceiling, into a pool at the floor that ran down into the river through a small opening. There was not enough room for a boat to pass through, but a person could.

"Were you able to wring anything from her Grace?" his brother asked, understanding full well how it had gone.

Rotham repeated the Duchess' words. "It fits the description, but where is Hope?"

"This is certainly a cold, damp, dark place," Carew agreed.

"It doesn't make sense," Gus said, obviously frustrated. "The water is shallow enough that we could see her now." All that was visible were some of the rocks that had fallen down.

"And you have checked every cave? There could be no hidden chambers?" he asked, stupidly, knowing they were as desperate as he.

Montford and Stuart were studying one of the carvings, and interrupted. "It appears that this drawing indicates the water level fluctuates."

"It looks as though a tide comes in, possibly with a full moon," Carew added, looking at another drawing.

"I thought only the sea ebbed and flowed with the tide," Max said.

"Evidently not. This shows the cavern completely filled with the full moon." Carew pointed to the drawing.

"Which means our time is limited. The Duchess suggested Hope would not survive until morning," Westwood said.

The fury in Max's blood turned to ice. "What else do the carvings show? There has to be some type of room here...some type of chamber in which she would be trapped and then drown when the water rose."

"Unless they are hidden under the water, we have found nothing!" Gus insisted.

"But have you looked behind the water?" Westwood asked.

Gus frowned, as if he thought Westwood were confused.

Rotham understood, and dashed towards the waterfall, his feet pounding through the water, sending splashes upwards as he neared the cascading waterfall that appeared to flow down the cavern wall.

Max plunged through the falling water, and began to grope at the wall. "There's a door!" It was difficult to see, as he had to reach through the water to feel it. When he found the handle and tried to turn it, the door was locked.

His curses echoed through the cavern. "Find Gilford quickly! Someone else go to Abernathy and someone to the Duke. I do not want any time wasted. One of them must have a key!"

Max banged on the door. "Hope! Hope! Are you in there?"

He frantically scrutinized the large, oaken door, urgency in his eyes, as the others hurriedly scoured for the key and tools.

"I think we could break these hinges, if needs be," Westwood said, appearing beside him and examining the door, too.

"We also might be able to jemmy the lock."

"It will be loud, but at this point that is the least of our worries."

The minutes ticked by as they waited, but Max would not leave Hope's side, just in case.

"She has to be in here, Dom. She has to be." His voice cracked as the fear inside him crept out.

Neither of them spoke about what the alternative would be if she'd been tossed into the river.

Gilford and Montford returned first. "I have no key, my lord, since the grotto was closed off."

Abernathy rushed in with Major Stuart to see if he could help. "I am afraid I have never had a key to this door, my lord."

Carew came back with some of the servants carrying tools, and they began to pound away at the steel hinges, which seemed to have forged together over time.

Each of them took turns at hammering and beating on the old, rusted iron. It was exhausting work, and the hinges barely seemed to budge. Soon they were all sore and sweating from a great deal of effort for very little progress. "Maybe we would have better luck splitting the wood," Carew suggested.

"Whatever it takes, but we must not stop!" Max ordered as he took a hammer and pounded at the door with frustration. It felt as though the door was as thick as a tree. Westwood was trying to insert a crowbar under the edge but chiselling away at the stone around the door was also very slow work.

Almost two hours had passed since they'd first discovered the hidden door and no one dared to give up.

"Where is the blacksmith? I fear he may be our last resort."

"Max!" Gus shouted as he came into the cavern with the Duke limping along beside him. "Here is the key!"

"Thank God!" Max was in such a hurry to take the key from his brother that it almost slipped from his hands into the pool below.

The Duke stayed only to ensure that the door opened. "Now I am off to banish the Duchess from these shores forevermore."

Max did not know if his father was attempting to be pithy, but so long as he never saw the woman again, he did not care where she went.

FRANTICALLY, Hope tried the door handle, but it would not budge. She banged on the door, then searched the room while she still had light, but there was nothing there. It was naught but an empty room. There were no tools or hidden keys to give her an opportunity to be a heroine like in the novels she and her sisters enjoyed reading, where they would save themselves. There was nothing romantic whatsoever about her current situation.

The more she dwelled on it, the worse was her anguish. She wrapped the blanket around her and sank down the wall to the floor, feeling as though she was sinking into a deep abyss. She tried to reason that Rotham would have noticed she was missing and would be searching for her, but would he even know of this place? It could be hours or days before anyone found her, and she was already damp and chilled to the bone. How long could a person survive like that? She was not certain she wished to know.

For a time, Hope tried to think about her sisters, and even Rotham. She had known only an hour's happiness before it had been stolen from her! It was hard to keep her thoughts from becoming morbid when she was so physically miserable. There was little to find comfort in when she was shaking so hard her teeth rattled. She put her hands under her arms and burrowed her face down into the blanket wrapped around her, but since her clothing was damp, it did very little to ease the cold.

Would the footman keep his word and come to visit her? He had not been rough or mean. But how long would that be? It was hard not to despair. Trusting in someone who would aid the Duchess, and put Hope in such a prison in the first place was foolish.

Having always been the one to try to live up to her name, she felt she had earned the right to thoughts of desolation in light of the Duchess's genuine effort to make her suffer. In this state, it was impossible for her soul not to feel utterly forsaken, weighed down by an insurmountable sense of sorrow. How could this end happily? She could think of no possible way. The future, which a short time ago had seemed brighter than the sun, was now looming as a bleak, dark hole.

How much time had passed? It felt to be an eternity already. She tried to stay awake to be alert for anyone who might possibly be searching, but exhaustion was overtaking her. Perhaps if she could sleep for just a little while, it would conserve the little strength she had left. She closed her eyes and allowed herself to slip into an abyss of darkness.

So deep in her state of despondency that she had become numb in body and spirit, she did not at first hear her rescuers.

A distant pounding resounded in the distance and Hope stirred a little, but she was too cold to move. It was easier to be still. The pounding became louder and harder, and she tried to open her eyes, but all she could see was darkness.

It sounded as though someone was calling to her from far away. Was she dreaming?

A loud bang was followed by a rush of air. Suddenly, light flooded her cell.

"Hope, my love, I am here." Rotham scooped her into his arms and the relief overwhelmed her.

"Max," she whispered.

"You are so cold! We must get you warm at once!" He lifted her and searing pain shot through her limbs.

She cried out a little, but he seemed to know what the problem was.

"She is here! We must warm her quickly!" he shouted to someone. He carried her out through the rushing water and she flinched as it hit her face. Moments later, Lord Westwood and Lord Augustus wrapped blankets about her as she lay cradled in Rotham's arms.

Rotham whisked her back to the house with breathtaking speed, his embrace so firm she found breath scarce, yet she uttered no protest. Relief flooded her, safe in his arms, as he whispered sweet endearments and vowed to shield her from harm eternally. He revealed that the Duchess had been banished from the estate, ensuring she would never plague them again.

Faith and her sisters were waiting in her chambers, a warm bath ready and waiting. The warm blankets had already gone a long way towards improving her circulation, and she knew the bath would warm her further.

"Thank God!" Faith exclaimed and she hugged Hope as Rotham gently set her down.

"We will help her from here, my lord," Faith said to Rotham. He gave a reluctant nod, and kissed Hope on the cheek.

"I will ring for you when she is more herself," Faith assured him.

Faith and her younger sisters quickly stripped the blankets and clothes from her and then helped her to step into the bath. It was excruciating as her body regained its normal temperature. Her sisters plied her with hot tea laced with brandy, and she shook as her body slowly warmed.

"Thank God this happened in the summer," Patience remarked.

"I don't want to imagine such a thing in the winter," Grace agreed.

"I cannot believe the Duchess ordered such a wicked thing!"

Hope said nothing. She did not want to think about that woman ever again. She herself had already gone through the process and real-ization over and over in her mind, but she understood her sisters' need to speak of it, so she said nothing. All her efforts were centred on regaining her warmth.

"I heard them say the Duke was himself escorting her from the property. He feels responsible for allowing her to go as far as this," Patience remarked.

"How could anyone have guessed she was mad?" Grace asked.

"Not mad," Hope whispered.

"It turns out that one of the footmen was the son of her Grace's maid. He was the one arranging the delivery of things unnoticed," Patience said. "According to Jenkins, the maid was so grateful to have been allowed to keep her position when she had a child, that she is now completely devoted to the Duchess."

"What of them?" Hope asked.

"Oh, they are gone as well. His Grace took them wherever he took the Duchess. Good riddance, I say," Patience emphasized.

"Would you like more warm water or are you ready to come out?" Faith asked Hope with a warning glance to her sisters.

"I should like to get out now." They quickly surrounded her with flannels, then blankets again. She would have laughed if she'd had the strength as she was helped into her bed, and then tucked in snugly with several more blankets.

"How are you feeling now, my dear?" Faith asked.

"Much better. I no longer feel as though I am being stabbed with thousands of needles."

Another warm tisane was placed into her hands, but she pushed it away.

"I am well enough now," she said with a shake of her head. "I am very fortunate that I was found so quickly, you know."

"We should let her rest," Faith said, and with a little grumbling, they all agreed. Each came over to give her a hug and a kiss before Faith ushered them out.

She closed the door behind them, and then came over to sit beside Hope on the bed. She opened her mouth to speak, then hesitated and closed it again.

"What is it?" Hope asked.

"Westwood and I were wondering if you would like to leave. I think you need time to heal before making any final decisions. It will be impossible to prevent a scandal, and you may find, after time to reflect, that this is not what you wish for."

Hope began to cry. Everything that had happened hit her at once and the thought of leaving Rotham was too much. She also thought it might be too much for him.

"Oh, Hope, forgive me. I did not mean to upset you. I should not have said anything," Faith remonstrated with herself as she pulled Hope into a hug.

Hope smiled weakly.

"You need to rest. Shall I leave you now?"

"As long as someone stays nearby. I know she has gone, but…"

"But of course, one of us will be here. You need only call."

"Please tell Rotham that I am unharmed." Hope turned and nestled into the pillow. It was hard to believe that it was really over.

CHAPTER 20

Max paced around the study, wondering what he could do next. It had been two days since Hope had last left her room. Was she lost to him forever because of his mother's high-handedness? That was a very mild way to phrase it, he reflected, considering the damage she had inflicted. Could it be overcome?

The Duke had still not returned from seeing the Duchess removed from the estate...yet another thing he needed to worry about. His father was hardly in any condition to be performing such a strenuous act, though Max could understand his wish to do it himself.

But what to do about Hope? Westwood had convinced Max to give her time, but it was killing him, inch by miserable inch. How could he make her feel safe again? At least she hadn't left Davenmere. Westwood had confessed that they had tried to convince her to do so, and she had refused. That was something.

He stopped pacing and stood by the window, looking out over the vast estate. It would soon be his, but it meant nothing without Hope.

He wished to send her a note—some communication of his regard —but due to her Grace's recent antics he feared they would be a distressing reminder instead of a welcome token of his affection.

There was a knock on the door, and he called for them to enter.

Perhaps it was finally news of the Duke. He waited for the person to speak, and when they didn't, he turned to look.

His breath caught when he saw Hope standing there just inside the doorway, watching him cautiously. He wanted to run to her with open arms, but somehow sensed it would be better to let her come to him.

Max smiled shyly at her. It was a strange sensation, but he was definitely feeling bashful for perhaps the first time in his life. "How are you?" What a ridiculous question! It did not even begin to encompass his concern for her well-being.

"I am well, sir. I asked Faith to tell you. Did she not?" She tilted her head to the side in the most endearing fashion.

"She did, but nothing compares to seeing you whole before me."

"Forgive me. I did not mean to cause you concern. I slept for almost one full day, I believe."

"You may have all the time in the world, so long as I know you are safe."

She stepped forward, and Max held out his arms. She ran into them, and he wrapped them tightly around her, inhaling the fresh lemon scent of her, wanting to be so close they became one.

"Oh, my Hope, I have been so afraid," he confessed.

"Afraid?" Her big blue eyes looked up at him, questioning.

"Yes. I have been afraid you would come to your senses and run far away from here and me forever."

"I must be out of my mind, then, because that is the last thing I wish to do."

"You are certain?"

"I have no doubts whatsoever that I want to spend the rest of my life with you, Max."

"What about the scandal?"

"I am certain there will be one, but we will pretend nothing is amiss. Eventually, people will either accept us as we are, or not. Our happiness lies together."

"Indeed, I cannot imagine being happy without you," he admitted, still holding her close.

"Do you wish to wait, now that your mother is no longer a concern?"

"Absolutely not. I did say that in order to flush out the offender, but my primary wish is to be married to you as soon as possible. Now I only ask that we wait for my father to return."

"Where has he gone?" He saw the realization across her face. "Oh, yes, I remember now. You said he was personally overseeing the Duchess' departure."

"Yes. I expect him back shortly. When you knocked, I thought it might be news of his return."

Hope pulled out of his arms. His first instinct was to pull her back, but he let her go.

"Have you considered that marrying quickly will compound the scandal?" she asked as she walked over to the window.

"I have discovered, in my nearly thirty years, that people who wish to make a scandal of something will do so regardless of what I do. With the circumstances being what they are, I have no wish to delay. If the Duke were to depart this life in the near future, that would mean an entire year before we could wed, and I cannot abide the thought of being parted from you for so long."

She turned and smiled at him. "I confess that would be a sore trial for me as well. And for all that I have been through to be with you, I do think my wishes matter."

"More than anything in the world." He did go to her then, and took her back into his arms. He covered her lips with his and struggled not to frighten her with his passion. However, he could not but let escape the fear he felt, and his desperate love for her, into the burning need he had to possess her—body, spirit, and mind. His need surpassed any other worldly consideration, and his love for her had only become more pressing with each obstacle they had been forced to overcome since their arrival at Davenmere.

Thankfully, Hope seemed to return his passion, at least, if not perhaps the same depth of feeling. He could only pray it were so. His first instinct was to crush her to him and never let her go.

To think he had ever thought her not well suited to the role of

Duchess of Davenmere, when she had shown her strength and poise in ways far superior to his mother. Max dismissed the thoughts, not wanting the witch to intrude upon these precious moments.

He lifted Hope and sat her on his lap, wanting to hold her and cherish her whilst he could still bridle his passions.

"I love you, Hope," he whispered into her ear. "I realize you may not yet share such feelings for me, but I can go not one moment longer without telling you."

She shook her head and turned to look at him.

"What is it? I am declaring my undying love to you and yet you shake your head. What must I do to convince you?"

"I shake my head because I cannot believe you doubt my love is at least equal to yours!"

"At least?" He feigned offence. "I can see you need more convincing." He crushed his mouth to hers before she had time to reply.

With difficulty, he controlled his desire and kissed her deliberately, taking his time and playfully teaching her, showering her with affection and the promise of what was to come. Hopefully, that would be a lifetime of mutual love and devotion.

After some time of appreciating her lips, eyes, ears, nose and cheeks, he drew back a little. She rested her head against his shoulder, a pose in which he was content to hold her forever.

"I almost forgot to give you this," he said as he pulled the betrothal ring from his pocket and slipped it on her finger. "I was going to give it to you when I found you missing that day."

"It is beautiful," she said as she admired it.

"It does not compare to you." He showered her with kisses to show her just how incomparable he thought her.

"I do not desire ever to leave your arms," she said wistfully.

"Your wish is my command. Shall I have everyone else sent away?"

She laughed. "I would not mind, but I suppose we should marry first."

He sighed heavily, as if much put upon. "I suppose we must. Do you think our sisters might have arranged it by now?"

"Knowing Faith, yes."

"Knowing Diana, she snapped her fingers, and it was so."

"We should go and ask them," she suggested.

"In a moment." He was in no hurry to relinquish his hold on her. "There is the small matter of having the banns called," he reminded her.

"Are dukes not above such insignificant details?" she teased.

"Technically, no, but in practical terms, yes. A word to an archbishop would be all that was necessary to procure a special licence."

"Let me guess. Your father is well acquainted with just such a one?"

"Of course. But with having had to deal with the Duchess' banishment, he might not have thought to ask for one. I do not think it will delay us long. I can also dash to London, procure one, and be back within a few days. If, that is, you would like to marry here. If you do not, I will understand."

"I assumed, given the state of your father's health, that it would be for the best. I imagine that escorting your mother away will have taxed not only his body but also his spirit."

He kissed Hope on the top of her head, filled with gratitude. "What did I ever do to deserve you? No, do not answer that. I have done nothing. However, I do realize I am the most fortunate man alive to have you for my bride."

"Indeed, you are, and I will never let you forget it," she said playfully, and on those words, drew his head down again to kiss her.

RELUCTANTLY, Hope left Max and went to find Faith and Diana. She could not exactly explain why she had stayed in her room for two days once she had recovered from her exhaustion. Nonetheless, it had then taken some time to realize the nightmare was truly over. But she had reflected deeply on what Faith had said about making certain marriage to Rotham was the right decision. Her reflections always returned to the thought that her life would be unimaginable without Rotham by her side. There would be scandal and difficulty, but with him, she would weather the storm.

Hope could not but smile as she walked along the corridors of the house. Whilst there was much to be sorry for, there was so much love and a beautiful future together to look forward to. Nothing would diminish that after what they had been through to be together.

She found Faith and Diana in one of the private family parlours, along with Patience, Grace, Joy, and Lady Claudia.

"Look at that smiling face," Faith remarked. "I am very happy to see it," her sister said as she moved forward to embrace her.

"What have you been doing?" Hope asked when she looked around and saw bouquets of flowers, place cards, and even plates of cake scattered about the room. Freddy Tiger was enjoying himself to Joy's piece.

"You did not imagine that we would not see to everything, surely? You may approve what we have done or you may leave the whole to us," Faith answered.

"Why not both? I may see what you have done and then leave the whole to you."

"One would think her Duchess already," Lady Diana said with a smile.

Hope tasted a bite of a moist, fluffy sponge that tasted of brandy and spices.

"Do you like it? It is Max's favourite, which we thought to have instead of a traditional bride cake, but we can order one of each if you prefer."

"No, no. This is divine," Hope said, and finished the piece given to her.

She could only approve of what the sisters had done for the quickly arranged wedding. Grace had created drawings of beautiful floral arrangements and candles to adorn the chapel, and the ballroom would have a similar design, allowed to flow into the formal gardens on the west lawn. It was more than she had ever dreamed of.

"How many guests do you expect?"

"Who knows, but it is not every day that the heir to Davenmere is married. We have invited everybody who is anybody, of course, but on such short notice I expect maybe half of them to attend," Lady Diana added casually.

"How many invitations have been sent out?" Hope was afraid to know the number, but asked anyway.

"A few hundred." She waved her hand in the air, as though it were an average London affair.

"I had hoped for something small and intimate."

"Becoming a duchess will require a slight shift in your thinking," Diana said kindly. "Having Max for a husband will be worth it. You will not be a duke and duchess behind closed doors…and he needs that—and you—very much."

As Hope needed him, she mused, trying not to reveal the direction of her thoughts as she recalled his caresses. She nodded, resolved not to complain. She knew what was expected of her. It would be a small price to pay.

"Excellent," Diana said cheerfully.

The butler knocked on the open door and addressed Lady Diana. "The Duke's carriage has been seen on the main drive, my lady."

"At last! Inform Lord Rotham, if you please." She stood up and to the room said, "Now we need not concern ourselves about changing the date. We may sample the champagne later." She winked at Hope's sisters, then walked over and kissed Hope on each cheek before she and Lady Claudia left the room to greet their father.

"I am glad his Grace has returned. Rotham has been extremely concerned about him."

"I take it that all is well with him?" Faith asked carefully. "We did wonder if this was a little premature, but Lady Diana insisted on beginning the arrangements." She waved her hand at all the wedding plans and preparations.

"All is well," Hope assured her sisters.

"I could have told you that by the smile on her face," Joy retorted.

Little Freddy was winding his way around her ankles. "No, Freddy, you may not pounce upon my train when I pass down the aisle," she teased.

"I will make certain he is on his lead this time," Joy said.

"He did not put me out," Faith said, bending over to pick up the cat and then scratching his ears.

Another knock caused them to turn about and see who was there. Rotham's imposing frame filled the doorway.

He smiled warmly at Hope, then nodded a greeting to her sisters. "My father has returned. Would you like to go with me to welcome him?"

"Yes, of course." She was touched beyond measure that he would think of her. He held out his arm to her, and she took it gladly. As they walked through the great hall, then the entrance towards the drive, she realized it would be one of many such times. It was awe-filling, looking at Davenmere in such a light. Each room so steeped in history, as well as each servant's face, bore the responsibility of a legacy that she and Max would build together. It was very humbling.

They walked out to the drive, where Lady Diana stood with Lady Claudia and Lord Augustus, waiting for the carriage to arrive.

However, when a vehicle came into view, there was not one, but three carriages.

"Whatever is this?" Max asked.

"It looks as though Father has brought back some wedding guests," Diana remarked.

"It would not surprise me in the least," Gus agreed.

The first carriage slowed to a stop, and Max went to open the door for his father and handed him out. He was looking weary and worn, but he still smiled at his son. Max helped him to climb down and Hope noticed he leaned heavily on a cane, but once he was firmly on the ground, he held out a hand to Hope. "Come, child."

Hope took his offered hand, and waited for him to speak.

"It is finished and you will never be troubled by my wife again. I can only convey my sorrow and apologies for not having dealt with her sooner."

"You could not have known, your Grace. I can only regret being the source of such...emotions within her."

"Never think the fault is yours, my dear. It lies entirely within her mind."

"Where have you taken her?" Max asked.

"It is probably better you do not know for now, my son. Now is a time for happiness. I want to put this matter behind us. Speaking of which, I have brought a surprise for you." He looked at the carriage which had drawn up behind them and the guests who were alighting.

Max grinned and looked at Hope. "Would you believe it? My father has brought an archbishop!"

"It was the best wedding gift I could think of," the Duke said and squeezed each of their hands before releasing them.

Hope laughed and could only shake her head as a pleasant-looking gentleman with grey hair and dark eyebrows stepped forward and they made their bows.

"Your Grace, this is my lovely bride, Miss Whitford," Max said. "Hope, may I present the Archbishop of York."

"Rotham would find the loveliest bride to be had in all of England," his Grace said.

"I am fortunate, indeed," Max agreed. "Welcome back to Davenmere. We are grateful to you for coming."

"I heard I missed a hunt! And in June!" the Archbishop exclaimed, known for almost turning down the archbishopric for fear of having to give up hunting. It certainly explained the friendship between him and the Duke.

"A capital run it was!" the Duke chimed in. "You must return in the autumn after the cubbing. It has been much too long!"

"It certainly has."

"You have something suitably grand planned, I trust, Diana?" Hope heard the Duke ask.

"It is best just to smile and let them have their way," Max whispered in her ear.

"I am coming to realize that," she agreed.

"Now, I wonder who is in the third carriage?" A black travelling coach pulled by four matching black horses waited for the door to be opened and the step lowered.

The arrivals were strangers to Hope. An older, but distinguished looking gentleman and a servant, likely his valet, alighted.

"Who is it?" she whispered to Rotham.

"I am not acquainted with him," he confessed.

When the Duke looked over at the guest, he ceased his conversation with his children. "Shall we go inside, and I will introduce you all. I think, perhaps, it will be best if your sisters are present."

Hope was utterly confused, but allowed Rotham to lead her into the drawing room. "Gilford, if you would send in the Whitford ladies," his Grace ordered.

Her sisters seemed as confused as she when they arrived, entering the room cautiously before sitting down.

The Duke smiled and spoke to Hope. "My dear, when you told me who you were, and that you had been orphaned, it surprised me that you had been brought up by a stranger and then given into Westwood's guardianship. It made me think that perhaps all of your Whitford family must have passed away. However, a few letters were sent at my direction and, as it happens, one of your paternal uncles is still living. I realize that you and Lady Westwood are now in a position to support your sisters, but thought you might value that connection." He indicated a distinguished gentleman, aged perhaps in his late fifties.

All her sisters seemed to turn at once to survey this relation they had not known about.

He walked over to them, and at once Hope recognized some of her father's familiar features, such as the bright blue eyes each of them had inherited. His hair and whiskers were black streaked with silver, and there were deep lines etched on his face, denoting a predisposition to laughter. This was probably what their father would have looked like had he lived.

"Ladies, may I present Admiral David Whitford."

The gentleman made them a bow. "Ladies, I am regretful that I lost contact with my brother and was thus unable to provide for you during your time of need, though it appears you have suffered no harm by my absence. I was also in the Navy and have but recently retired and returned home. Regretfully, the news of my brother's death did not reach my ears until I returned to England. I remained a bachelor as it was a difficult life to take a wife. I do hope that now you will, at the very least, be able to spare a little time for your old uncle."

Hope walked to him and took his hands. She kissed each cheek. "I could not be more pleased to know that you still live, sir. Father was given to speak well of you."

Her sisters also greeted him, and while they did so, Hope went to the Duke. "Thank you, sir," she said as she kissed his cheek. "I cannot imagine a more wonderful gift."

CHAPTER 21

Less than a fortnight from when Max had first issued the request to Diana to plan his wedding, the day had now arrived. The last few weeks had felt more like years under the weight of his mother's disgraceful behaviour. It had taken a definite toll on his father and all of the gains he had initially made seem to have been erased by the banishment of the Duchess.

However, the Whitford sisters were a continual delight to their new-found uncle, and they seemed genuinely to enjoy each other's company. They had climbed the peaks, gone riding and fishing, and attended the village fair with him.

Since Hope had been too busy with preparations for the wedding to spend as much time with Admiral Whitford and her sisters, Max determined to make certain the gentleman was invited for a visit after their wedding trip, which would not take place until after the Duke had passed away.

Max wanted every last moment with his father, even though it would have surprised him to say so but a month ago. He would be forever grateful for this time with him. Max could only hope the Duke would live long enough to see his first grandchild from his son.

Davenmere had been transformed from a cold, uninviting castle into a warm, happy place full of life. Every room at Davenmere and in every nearby village was filled with guests.

Max walked through the house to the ballroom and reception rooms where the festivities would take place. He was not surprised that such a miracle had been wrought. His sisters and Hope's had been determined to make everything perfect.

He chuckled as he surveyed the ballroom. The sisters had chosen to elaborate on the Roman theme, but it felt as a nod to the ball where the Whitford sisters had made their debuts as angels in the heavens. It was where he had first danced with Hope.

Harps and lyres had been placed around the room to provide the music of the gods, and white carnations had been arranged in clusters to resemble clouds. The ballroom doors opened out on to the view of the waterfall, and the sun was bright and clear, as if the heavens were watching and approved.

Lavish displays of pastries and desserts had already been carefully arranged, including a beautifully iced three-tiered cake with tiny, pale yellow jonquils arranged in small bunches around the top and sides.

It felt as though a weight had been lifted from the house following the Duchess' absence. It was a sad testimony to her legacy, he reflected, that the duchy was the better for her removal from it. Nothing whatever must shadow his happiness in wedding Hope, and despite their beginning with a tragedy, Max was determined it would not overshadow the future.

Hurried footsteps approached. "Here you are, at last! I have been searching all over the house for you," Gus said, in a scolding tone. "Diana has ordered us to take you to the chapel at once."

Max turned with a smile. "I have not been hiding from you."

"*Touché*," Gus said appreciatively, as Max echoed his brother's earlier words.

Carew, Montford, and Freddy followed him into the room. "Growing sentimental?" Carew asked.

How the devil did he know? "Simply reflecting on the tortuous path we have taken to arrive at this day, and rejoicing that it appears to be behind us. With luck, we have now reached better going."

Gus slapped him on the back in a commiserating, brotherly way.

"My friends, you are falling like the French at Waterloo," Carew said. "Even Monty is being chased in his dreams by the sounds of wedding bells."

Montford smiled as though he welcomed such a thing.

"Do not look at me." Freddy held up his hands.

"Just wait," Max warned. "Your day shall come."

Freddy denied this vehemently.

"We had best be going," he said, looking at his lifelong friends, each one dressed in their finest attire. They had all chosen shades of cream and grey for coats and breeches, with varying pastels for their waistcoats to match the shades the Whitford sisters were wont to wear.

"I am grateful all of you are here. It means a great deal to me." He tried not to choke on his emotion and shook his head. "I am become mawkish."

A few of them cleared their throats, evidently sharing his sentiment. "We should go. It would not do to delay the wedding due to my sensibilities."

They left the house by the eastern path through the pine wood. It was the least travelled one for the guests, as the estate chapel was nestled up above the rest of the estate—nearer to God, he reckoned, permitting himself a wry smile. There was a chapel within the house for the family and servants to use for daily prayers, but it was too small to accommodate such a grand gathering. A more circuitous carriageway had been laid in the last century, so those who did not care to walk could be driven in one of the open landaus.

"I have not been to the chapel in an age," Gus remarked. "In fact, probably not since Diana was married."

"I remember the time we were caught stealing the biscuits prepared for a party of guests and we ran up here to hide," Freddy said.

"How long did it take them to find you?" Montford asked.

"We gave ourselves up when it grew dark. A chapel is a scary place with all the crypts and tombs."

He shuddered even now at the thought. Max noticed and laughed.

"We did not learn our lesson well. One holiday, when the grooms were busy, we slipped out on some of the Duke's prized hunters, and when discovered we tried to escape here, but the game was up."

"Oh, but it was worth it. Those were the sweetest goers I've ever had the pleasure of mounting," Freddy said wistfully, as though he were a green lad of sixteen again.

"I was with you that time," Carew remembered. "To this day I can feel the thrashing we took. But it did inspire me to breed horses just like those."

"I thought you were with us that time, Monty," Max said, trying to recall which of his friends had indulged in the prank.

"He was, but he would not take the hunters out with us," Freddy said with a scowl at Montford as though he was still unforgiven. "You may be thinking of Westwood. He was there as well."

"Have you ever done anything you were not supposed to, Monty?" Freddy asked reproachfully.

"Why is that a reason for scorn? It is an admirable trait!" he argued.

"It must be so then," Carew mocked, and clapped him on the back.

"You also teased me at the time. I still do not regret my choice."

The other fellows exchanged amused glances.

They reached the narrow stone staircase that led up to the chapel in the woods, as they referred to it, and ascended it one at a time. At the top, set within a garden, stood several statues of martyred saints, which looked battered and mournful.

"These are the only statues my ancestors allowed that were not Roman gods," Max pointed out in a sardonic tone as he held out his hand to the sculptures.

"At least they had some sense not to blaspheme on holy ground," Gus agreed.

The chapel was a masterpiece, and as it sat overlooking the estate, provided a sanctuary in the wood.

Inside, the walls were of stone lined with stained glass scenes of Jesus' teachings. The altar was a gruesomely accurate carving of Jesus on the cross, and the ceiling boasted a painting of the ascension to heaven.

They were the first to arrive, although a handful of servants were attending to last-minute details, such as lighting the candles at the end of each pew and near the altar, thus giving the inside a warm glow.

Suddenly Max grew nervous, which was absurd. He was certain this was what he wanted, more than anything. He listened to his friends continuing to tease each other, and he tried to smile, but the waiting was excruciating.

At last, the guests began to arrive. Major Stuart and Captain Fielding had returned with Colonel Renforth. Max knew Patience would be pleased about that. A few of the local gentry took their places, and then as many members of the House of Lords as the chapel would hold, apparently. How the devil had Diana arranged that so quickly?

Lord and Lady Wilton arrived with Lady Agatha, but Lady Matilda was conspicuously absent. Her behaviour would have been amusing if not for the circumstances threatening Hope at the time. Lord Brosner and Lady Alice had returned for the ceremony as well. Max hoped there were no ill feeling as he knew Brosner had wanted Hope for himself, but all was fair in love, after all.

There seemed to be an interminable pause in arrivals, and Max was hard put not to pace about while he waited. Carriage wheels sounded, signalling the rest of the party, and at last his family was shown in. The Duke was dressed in his finest court regalia, and though it hung loosely about him, his smile detracted from the fact. Diana and Claudia discreetly supported him on either side as Lord Courtenay followed behind. The doors closed behind them and Max knew the time had come.

The organ began to play, and footmen swung the doors open again. Then began a procession of the four lovely Whitford sisters, who, to the unacquainted eye, could have been mistaken one for the other, so similar were they. To his surprise, Joy, with her scar and mischievous twinkle in her eyes, came first, making him wonder if the little cat would make an appearance. He had little doubt the animal would be there. The more demure Grace came next, followed by the practical Patience, and lastly Faith, Lady Westwood. They stood near the altar, opposite his friends, as Lord Westwood escorted Hope down the aisle of the nave. A more beautiful sight he'd never beheld. He was most humbled that she'd chosen him, yet a rare smile that transformed his whole face delighted those fortunate enough to see it. There was no doubt amongst those present that day that both Lord and Lady Rotham had found one of those rare love matches.

SOMEHOW, Hope could not reconcile that this was real. It felt as though she were floating on air and walking through a dream. There had been so many obstacles to this match that it had seemed impossible. Yet here they finally were.

Some kind of miracle had been performed to bring a modiste in all haste from London. Lady Diana had called in some favours, for that Hope knew, though that lady claimed anyone would be happy to put themselves out for the privilege of designing for the next Duchess of Davenmere.

Her gown was an incredible creation in the palest cream and gold silk, which was covered in exquisite Brussels lace with shining gold threads and tiny pearls interwoven through it. The Davenmere parure of white and gold diamonds had been delivered to her chamber that morning, and she adorned as the final touch.

She almost felt like a duchess.

An open landau, pulled by matching white horses, was waiting for her. Faith and Westwood were to accompany her, as another carriage was to convey Patience, Grace, and Joy, escorted by their uncle.

It was perhaps a mile to the chapel in the woods, but the path was curvy and steep, so the horses were kept to a walk.

The chapel was nestled in the trees and seemed almost a smaller version of St. Paul's in its grandeur. She scarcely had time to assimilate its architecture, but the sculptures, paintings and stained glass were exquisite. She decided she would return very soon, to study every detail, but now her attention was all upon her groom. Her sisters walked down the aisle, where Rotham stood with his closest friends to support him. As her uncle had just entered their lives, she decided Westwood would escort her down the aisle. She gazed solely at Max, so she would not have to think about so many strangers watching her. Uncharacteristically, he was smiling widely at her and she almost stumbled from the unabashed pride he wore on his face. It was all for her. A rush of emotion nearly overcame her as tears of humility and gratitude filled her eyes. How had she ever thought she could marry another?

The archbishop began the service, and she scarcely heard a word he said once Rotham took her hand. The ceremony felt interminable, with six prayers and as many hymns. The vows, however, she did remember. The tender way Max looked at her and spoke each word made her feel cherished and worshipped.

Wilt thou have this woman to thy wedded wife, to live together after God's ordinance in the holy estate of matrimony? Wilt thou love her, comfort her, honour, and keep her in sickness and in health? And forsaking all other keep thee only to her, so long as you both shall live?

Max looked directly into her eyes. "I will."

Wilt thou have this man to thy wedded husband, to live together after God's ordinance, in the holy estate of matrimony? Wilt thou obey him, and serve him, love, honour, and keep him, in sickness and in health? And forsaking all other keep thee only unto him, so long as you both shall live?

Hope found her voice. "I will."

Who giveth this woman to be married unto this man?

Westwood stepped forward with Hope's sisters. "Her sisters and I."

Hope barely held her composure, then, as she turned to look at each of her beloved siblings. A few tears somehow managed to escape down her cheek. She turned back to Max and he wiped gently at the tears and held her face as he spoke his vows.

"I, Maximus, take thee Hope to my wedded wife, to have and to hold from this day forward, for better, for worse, for richer, for poorer, in sickness, and in health, to love, and to cherish, till death us depart, according to God's holy ordinance, and thereto I plight thee my troth."

Then it was her turn to repeat his words, after which he turned to his brother for the ring. He placed the gold band on her finger, then rubbed his thumb back and forth over her bare skin in a reassuring manner.

"With this ring I thee wed: this gold and silver I give thee: with my body I thee worship: and with all my worldly goods I thee endow. In the name of the Father, and of the Son, and of the Holy Ghost. Amen."

The rest of the ceremony was less coherent, although she did register when the Archbishop pronounced them man and wife. Max took her hand and placed a kiss in her palm, which felt more like a sacred promise than any words they had spoken.

The Archbishop performed their first Holy Communion as a married couple, whereupon they signed the Register and walked back down the nave to greetings and congratulations from the congregation.

They were not yet free of their obligations, however. It seemed many of the villagers had arrived outside to catch a glimpse of the proceedings, and as Hope and Max left the chapel, they were blessed with cheers and a shower of seeds and rice.

As they entered the carriage to return to the house for their wedding breakfast, in their turn, Max and Hope showered the villagers with vails. Then he delighted the crowd with an exuberant kiss on the lips for his fair bride, to many shouts and cheers of approval.

As they drove back down the carriageway to the manor, Max stole another kiss or two.

"Mine at last," he whispered as he placed a kiss on her ear. "What say you we forget our guests and skip the breakfast?" he asked in a scandalous voice. "They will not notice our absence anyway. I saw how many bottles of champagne were laid out for the occasion."

Hope laughed. "Perhaps we need not stay long, but I am afraid they might notice if we do not arrive at all."

"They will only think me wise beyond measure that I took you away."

"I am anxious for us to be alone as well, but you know we must at least greet everyone. Many of the guests have travelled a great distance, and your father is not equal to the task alone."

That sobered Max for a moment, even though she knew he had not been serious.

"If needs must." He sighed dramatically, then kissed her again, filling her with the promise of what was yet to come.

The receiving line was interminable, even though everyone was kind and genuine in their wishes. It was something that had to be endured. However, the gown and diamonds were very heavy and weighed her down.

"How many more are there?" he asked. "I long to waltz with you."

Hope smiled. "We are behaving like recalcitrant children, are we not? I was wishing I might change out of this gown."

"It is not that I am not grateful, but I am growing impatient. We have earned our time together."

"Indeed we have, and we will have each other for the rest of our lives."

"You are not encouraging me to behave, wife."

"A little while longer, dearest," she said, to herself as much as to him, keeping him at his post until the last guest had been welcomed.

The Duke had managed to stay on his feet during the receiving line, but Hope could sense him wilting next to her. "I must thank you, your Grace," she said, taking his arm and gently leading him to his seat.

"Father, if you please," he said with a smile as they walked, and Max came to his other side.

Hope smiled up at him. "Father. I do not know why you championed me, but I will never forget it."

He squeezed her arm gently as they reached his seat. He turned and spoke softly. "All I ask is you love him well, my dear. Life as a duke can be lonely, and I want more for him than I ever dared to have for myself." He looked away and cleared his throat. "Now, go and dance with your husband. Then you can give me a grandson." He winked at her.

"As you wish, Father."

Max led her to the centre of the ballroom floor and took her in his arms as the stringed instruments began to strum. "In my arms at last." He pulled her close into the movements of the dance and not once took his eyes from Hope's face. They moved as one in perfect harmony as she looked into his dark, chocolate eyes. Everyone else in the room faded into the background as they declared their love for one another with actions as they had in the chapel with words.

Others began to take the floor around them. Hope noticed Patience dancing with Major Stuart and wondered if there might be more than friendship on his part. She was quite certain of her sister's feelings.

"What did my father say to you?" Max finally asked.

She debated keeping the words to herself. It felt almost as if her own father had been speaking to her through the duke. "He told me to love you well."

"Words of wisdom that I intend to fulfil until my last breath."

Hope looked up to see his intense gaze, and the sincerity in his words.

"As do I," she vowed back.

"Now that I have found you, Hope, I will never let you go."

It was a year to the day from Max and Hope's wedding, and Davenmere was full of friends and family again, but this time for a very different reason. They had come to celebrate the birth and christening of the future heir to the dukedom, Lord Magnus Sylvester Valerius.

His namesake was still with them, and could not be more delighted that he had lived to see this day.

Currently, the doted upon child was in his namesake's arms, and the Duke was cooing and talking nonsense before an attentive, wide-eyed audience.

"Will the rest of us ever have the opportunity to hold him?" Patience asked grudgingly.

Hope laughed. "When his Grace rests."

"I have never seen a man so besotted with a babe," Faith mused.

"Some might think it beneath the dignity of a Duke, but he says Sylvester has given him a new reason to live."

"I suppose we can hardly begrudge him that," Patience conceded, "but I will hold my nephew before I leave!"

"Soon you will have another niece or nephew to dote on," Faith told her sisters. "If all goes well, by Christmas we expect to have another christening to attend."

"Oh, Faith!" Hope exclaimed. She and her sisters immediately hugged their eldest sibling.

Hope knew her sister had been despairing over the fact she had not yet conceived. It was joyous news indeed.

"I believe it is time we proceeded to the church," said his Grace, "We do not want to be late."

They drove in procession to the church and watched as Magnus Sylvester Valerius was christened, with Lord and Lady Westwood named as godparents. When Sylvester objected to the water, the Duke immediately took him from the bishop's arms, and his grandfather somehow seemed to entrance the child, causing him to forget why he was crying. Soon Sylvester was cooing and blowing bubbles at his Grace. It was not often that the future duke fussed. He was a joy to the entire household.

After the christening, Hope had ordered a picnic luncheon set up for them alongside the river.

It was a warm, sunny afternoon, too hot for anything other than relaxing in the shade with a cool glass of lemonade.

The Duke was seen napping with his grandson on his chest beneath the shade of an old chestnut.

Max and Hope sat on a swing overlooking the water.

"Are you happy, my love?" Max asked.

"I am happy and content," Hope answered. "Your father still lives, I love you more every day that passes, and my family is here with us to celebrate our precious child."

"That does paint the perfect picture," he agreed.

"Mm," she murmured as she laid her head on his shoulder, enjoying the slight breeze drifting off the water.

"Father has asked me for a favour," Max said, causing her to turn her head up to look at him.

"What is it?" she urged.

"He desires a trip to the Continent."

Hope did not know what to say.

"He makes a good argument," Max continued. "He has not been there since his Grand Tour and wishes to enjoy the warm sea air."

"If his doctor thinks it safe for him to travel, I daresay it could prove very beneficial, but how long would he be gone?"

"That is the minor detail I wish to discuss with you."

"Yes?"

"He wishes me to bring Sylvester and you and accompany him. You know he dotes on Sylvester and does not wish to be away from him for even a day. Dr. Cafferty has no objections. In fact, he thinks it might be good for him. Since you have never been to the Continent, I thought you might enjoy a visit to France and perhaps Italy."

"Indeed I should, husband—but to do so with a baby? Would it not put our son at risk?"

"We will take an army of servants to tend his every need. I think you would enjoy it. Manners on the Continent are less…restrained, shall we say?"

"I have always wished to travel. If Dr. Cafferty has no objections, then I think we should grant his Grace this wish. Thus far we have an excellent record of fulfilling them, do we not?"

"Indeed we do." Max chuckled. "I wonder what he will ask for next."

"Thus far I have been happy to oblige him. It is the least we can do for him when it was his support which enabled us to be together."

It was a solemn reminder of those tumultuous weeks before their wedding. The Duchess was never spoken of within hearing of the Duke, Max, or Hope. Her portrait had been removed to a remote attic, and replaced with one by Lawrence of Max and Hope together. Hope found it very humbling that Max had chosen her over the Davenmere name, and she intended to do everything in her power to bring him joy. She was happier than her wildest dreams could have imagined.

AFTERWORD

Author's note: British spellings and grammar have been used in an effort to reflect what would have been done in the time period in which the novels are set. While I realize all words may not be exact, I hope you can appreciate the differences and effort made to be historically accurate while attempting to retain readability for the modern audience.

Thank you for reading *Finding Hope*. I hope you enjoyed it. If you did, please help other readers find this book:

1. This ebook is lendable, so send it to a friend who you think might like it so she or he can discover me, too.

2. Help other people find this book by writing a review.

3. Sign up for my new releases at www.Elizabethjohnsauthor.com, so you can find out about the next book as soon as it's available.

4. Come like my Facebook page www.facebook.com/Eliza bethjohnsauthor or follow on Instagram @Ejohnsauthor or feel free to write me at elizabethjohnsauthor@gmail.com

ALSO BY ELIZABETH JOHNS

Surrender the Past

Seasons of Change

Seeking Redemption

Shadows of Doubt

Second Dance

Through the Fire

Melting the Ice

With the Wind

Out of the Darkness

After the Rain

Ray of Light

Moon and Stars

First Impressions

The Governess

On My Honour

Not Forgotten

An Officer Not a Gentleman

The Ones Left Behind

What Might Have Been

Leap of Faith

ACKNOWLEDGMENTS

There are many, many people who have contributed to making my books possible.

My family, who deals with the idiosyncrasies of a writer's life that do not fit into a 9 to 5 work day.

Dad, who reads every single version before and after anyone else—that alone qualifies him for sainthood.

Anj, who takes my visions and interpret them, making them into works of art people open in the first place.

To those friends who care about my stories enough to help me shape them before everyone else sees them.

Heather and Scott who help me say what I mean to!

And to the readers who make all of this possible.

I am forever grateful to you all.

www.ingramcontent.com/pod-product-compliance
Lightning Source LLC
Chambersburg PA
CBHW061348310726
48974CB00001B/253